I AM MAGGIE

VOLUME 01

BELINDA CRAWFORD

HENDRIX & FAUST
PUBLISHERS

Published by Hendrix & Faust, Publishers in 2025
Text copyright © Belinda Crawford 2025

www.belindacrawford.com

ISBN: 978-0-6459318-6-0 (ebook)
ISBN: 978-1-7641160-0-8 (paperback)

This is a work of fiction. Names, characters, businesses, places, events, locales, and incidents are either the products of the author's imagination or used in a fictitious manner. Any resemblance to actual persons, living or dead, or actual events is purely coincidental.

PRINTED AND BOUND BY INGRAMSPARK.
Australia: Ingram Content Group AU Pty Ltd, Melbourne, Victoria. US: Lightning Source LLC, La Vergne, Tennessee / Allentown, Pennsylvania / Jackson, Tennessee, United States. UK: Lightning Source UK Ltd, Milton Keynes, United Kingdom. Europe: Lightning Source UK Ltd, with facilities in Germany, France, and Spain.

The authorized representative in the European Economic Area is Lightning Source France, 1 Av. Johannes Gutenberg, 78310 Maurepas, France.
compliance@lightningsource.fr

CONTENTS

INTRODUCTION

I read a book (I won't tell you which one) and it made me want to write a story about a character who gets sucked into a computer game and has to go on an epic treasure hunt.

So I did.

Of course, me being me and chronically incapable of stopping at just *one* story; I decided to create a series out of it.

Initially, I was going to be sneaky and not tell anyone the stories were connected because, well… spoilers. Anyway, there was a reason—which may or may not have something to do with Maggie, Getty and Mae (totally has something to do with them)—and it was all going to be epic and as the reader slowly came to realise that *Don't Die, Spirit in the Sky* and the others were a series, [REDACTED] would [REDACTED].

sigh

Unfortunately, I can't keep a secret that juicy and so here we are with the first five Maggie stories together in a single volume. You may have read four of them in various instalments of *Short Bits*, but the fifth (*Vacant Spaces*) is exclusive to this collection.

Before I wrote *Vacant Spaces*, I wasn't sure how I wanted the Maggie series to play out, but the story was a turning point. I hope you like it.

Happy reading,
Belinda

I AM MAGGIE #1

DON'T DIE

'Maggie, hurry.'

'Yeah, Maggie. Hurry.'

The voices followed her into the Sphere. They echoed in the endless black space ringing in her ears and stabbing her heart, the first one was small and high, rich with fear, the other deep and mocking, amusement dripping from every syllable.

She hated that voice. Hated and feared it.

'Maggie, hurry.' It was Usha's voice that swirled through her skull though, Usha's fear that made her heart clench and her palms sweaty; was the only reason she didn't rip the VR helmet from her head and leap out of the couch for the other's throat.

Hurry. As if that echo were a trigger, a clock appeared front centre of her vision, casting bright blue highlights across the floor.

Sixteen hours, twenty-nine minutes.

Not enough time, the small, desperate other part, sweaty and achy with Usha's fear, whispered. And too much time, a whole six hours past the redline.

But all the time she had, the larger part said, the part that clenched her fists tighter and imagined pounding them into the other's face.

All the time she had, and none of it to waste, not even if her neutrons fried in the process.

A thought, and the Sphere came to life.

A featureless, sexless doll shunted the countdown aside.

Sixteen hours, twenty-seven minutes.

Options spinning through the void – race, gender, height hair, boobs, build – a deep melodic voice reaching up through the floor, spinning a tale of ancient gods and a mighty war, of spaceships and planets and the cataclysmic clash of science and magic. So many choices, so little time, and why the *fuck* had the bastard dropped her here, in the insane mess of the System's core, where anything and everything was possible?

No time to curse, no time to choose. All that mattered was Usha, the fear and hope in her eyes, the desperation in her voice.

Hurry.

Hurry, hurry, hurry.

A thought, the Sphere pulsing in acknowledgement and a glittering hundred-sided die hovered in the space before her.

// Randomise?

Yes.

// Confirm.

They'd told her to throw a random character even though she'd argued, begged them, even with the gun at Usha's head, perhaps because of it. She'd pleaded with them to let her choose a race and class she was good at, they'd said no, said they'd had plans.

She could throw it now, should think 'no' and complete the quest in half the time. Half the time she still didn't have.

She could almost hear the *snick* of the old-fashioned gun held to Usha's head as it charged.

// Confirm, the AI prompted again.

Confirm.

The featureless doll blurred, a hundred different voices, a hundred different shoulders and toes and tails, wings, horns, scales, bipedal, quadrupedal, blue skin, brown skin, white skin, all cycling in the space of a dozen heartbeats.

She felt each one against her chest, pounding in time to the seconds slipping from the clock.

Hurry.

Hurry.

Hurry.

A tingle ran through the Sphere, static fuzzing the doll in its endless spin. Something was wrong. A system error? A virus? The other's plan?

A pale, electric-blue shape writhed under her feet.

The spinning stopped, a new prompt appearing over the dice.

// Accept?

She didn't even look.

Accept.

A chorus filled her ears, lifted her from the floor and filled her skin with light. She was no longer standing on the edge of the Sphere looking in, but in its middle. Her hands ended in thick, pointed nails, the shadow of horns erupted from her brow and curled past her ears.

The chorus faded, the light no longer spilling from her pores, and she was lowered to the ground. Not the dark, reflective surface of the Sphere but the hard, white flagstones of Central, in the midst of the busiest place in the game. And, oh shit, perhaps she should have looked before accepting, because her feet weren't feet but talons and there was a weight on her back, the sense of new bones and musculature, and if she thought about it, twitched her shoulder blades just so—

SHHWAP.

Fuck.

Wings.

Wings plus horns plus talons… She put her hands to her chest, felt the cold steal, the delicate etching of feathers across its surface.

No.

Of all the races, all the classes, why the one that only spawned on random, that could be looted from a player's corpse?

A chuckle, malice dripping from every pulse of air against her eardrums. 'Like it, Maggie? We rigged the System just for you.'

The shiver running through the Sphere.

'You hacked the randomiser.' It was a growl, half-whispered and yet the words echoed in the virtual space and the avatars that had clustered around, the screenshots she can almost *feel* being taken of the Valkyrie in their midst, faltered.

How long before she was plastered across the fashion wars forums? How long before whatever anonymity she might have possessed was gone?

She looked up, over the massive square that was Central, and the sea of faces staring back. 'You're going to get me killed.'

'Then your girlfriend's gonna get dead too, Maggie. Besides,' he continued. 'It's easier to hack the randomiser than the quest, and with that skin, it's guaranteed to pop.'

Sixteen hours, twenty-four minutes.

*// **All or Nothing initiated.** Congratulations User990906134, you have been selected to participate in* All or Nothing. *Follow the clues, defeat your opponents and claim the World.*

// Death, logout or setting your status to AFK will result in automatic forfeiture.

Double fuck.

As she stood, frantically trying to calm her racing heart, with the whole world gawking at her, and *his* voice played in her ears – 'Gonna get *dead*, Maggie' – the non-combatant tag in the top right of her HUD disappeared, a new notification taking its place.

// PvP enabled.

A firebolt hit her in the chest.

⸙

One good thing about rolling a Valkyrie, it came with armour right off the bat. The firebolt left her scorched, health bar flashing a frantic dance of red but with enough life left to flap her monstrous raven-dark wings and get the hell out of dodge.

One bad thing about being a Valkyrie, she was fucking easy to spot, and even if none of the other low-level avatars had flight, the higher-level ones did.

She'd have been better off on the ground, with the fire-throwing mage.

'Inventory,' she yelled against the wind.

The HUD changed, a grid overlaying the cloud-shrouded mountains below. A rusty dagger, three level-one health potions and a pebble filled three of the ten slots.

She equipped the dagger, felt the weight of it, the cool ridges of leather-wrapped metal as it appeared in her hand. Took time to note the nicks in the blade, the mottled orange-brown of rust creeping outwards from the join between blade and hilt, the grime-encrusted remnants of what were once fine engravings on the spine, before she spun.

The closest purser took the dagger in his throat.

// Critical hit. Stun. Bleeding.

Their health bar flashed, a quarter chunk of it disappearing in the blink of an eye.

More opponents darkened the clouds behind them, wings in black and white and flaming green whipping up a storm, while jet boots and hoverboards left streaks of light in their wake. Some of the figures fought each other, swords, arrows, lasers and lightning arching through the sky.

Maggie kicked the knight from her blade, watching only long enough to ensure he tumbled in the direction of her next-closest pursuer, before plunging into the clouds below.

❧ ❦

She hid in the mountains, landing in the midst of a tiny clearing, her left wing clipping the edge of the thick canopy, turning her wobbly glide into an inelegant tumble.

// Damage. Environment. -40 health points.

A red flash on her HUD and when she focused, half her health bar was gone.

'Shit.' She heaved herself to her feet, trying to spit the taste of dirt from her mouth, and not fall over at the same time. 'Fuck.'

Having fucking bird claws where her feet should be would take some getting used to.

She glanced upwards, through the thick crosshatch of branches, leaves turning yellow and red, some fluttering down around her. Nothing but pale grey clouds playing with the tops of the tallest trees, not a hint of blue or sky or pursuit—

A swirl in the pale grey, too tight and too violent for a gust of wind, but just right for someone diving through the clouds.

She dove for the shelter of deeper forest, cursing the three-toed claws that caught in the soft dirt and the wings that defied every expectation of how a human should move. She held one tight against her back, while the other dragged.

A bright red nimbus covered the main bend of the dragging wing – so graceful in flight and so very *fucking* inconvenient now.

Fuck. Fuck. Fuck. Why hadn't she *checked* before she accepted the roll?

What would she have done if she had?

Too late to ponder it now, only time to ignore the pain blossoming in her side, the steady drop in health every time she brushed the injured appendage against a tree or bumped into a stone.

Sixteen hours, thirteen minutes.

Fuck the countdown, if any of the winged elites above caught her – *fuck*, if any of the winged *noobs* caught her – she was dead.

Dead. Dead. Dead.

'Dead as a dolphin, Maggie,' Dulton whispered right next to her real ear. The rancid small of his breath wound under the VR hood. 'If you don't hurry the *fuck* up.'

'I've got sixteen hours—'

'And a target on your winged arse. It's all over the forums, hotshot. The big boys want your shit.' She felt him lean closer, tried not to shudder as his lips brushed her ear. 'We didn't arrange all this for you not to last the time it takes to pop the noob cap baby but if you don't, your girl is gonna pay the price. Now move!'

She moved, crashing through forest not meant for beings with wings, then the edge of the game map.

The edge of the map.

How the fuck?

The edge of the game map wasn't just a line on a bit of virtual paper, it was the edge of the *world*. No more trees, no more mountains, no more ones and zeroes telling the electrons which coloured pixel to put where, just a solid wall and then nothing.

Except this wasn't nothing, there was grass beneath her claws, the rough bark of an ancient redwood under her hand, a warm trickle of sunlight on her face and a vibration against her hip.

She put her hand to it, found the stiff leather of a pouch. Her inventory appeared on the HUD.

The rusty knife was in the sheath on her thigh, leaving just the stack of health potions and the pebble occupying the ten meagre spaces.

The pebble was pulsing.

One, two, three. A pause. One, two, three.

She summoned it to her hand.

One, two, three.

It nestled within her palm, an unremarkable mottled grey, neither rectangular nor egg-shaped but slightly triangular, edges rounded in the way only a river rock tumbled by decades of water could be. If it weren't for the roundness, she could have dropped it where she stood and lost it amid the stones at her feet.

It pulsed again, the sensation running through her bones, from her fingers to the tips of her deadly sharp talons.

She concentrated on it.

More information.

// A river stone.

No longer just a pebble, as it had been before, but no more information either. Not a hint, a cryptic clue or an asterisk to suggest this pebble was more than what it appeared. Nothing save the pulse.

That, and the secret, off-map environment it chose to pulsate within.

But it was a river stone.

She needed to find a river, needed to find it fast.

Maggie looked up.

The canopy was dense but the spaces between the trees had grown with the height and girth of the trunks and even if she couldn't make it all the way through the green roof, perhaps she could take advantage of the highway of branches above.

Angry red still clung to the joint of her wing but a health potion would take care of that.

She summoned one to her hand, leaving just two, drank and felt the cooling tingle of magic rushing under her skin, knitting the hollow bones in her wing. A second and the job was done, her health bar flashing full.

Maggie launched herself into the air.

Three hard flaps, each one stirring a mini tornado, and she was perched atop a thick branch, claws digging into the hard wood like it was butter, wings half-spread for balance. The spaces here were tighter, with overlapping branches a half-metre thick and smaller offshoots spreading palm-sized leaves in the air. Still, now that she was here...

She scanned the green-tinged gloom, following the path of branches, the way sunlight filtered through the heavy leaves, highlighting certain sections over others. Almost like streetlamps. Convenient. Just like the way the next branch flowed from the one she stood on, a little too evenly spaced and a little too straight to be natural, without the bends and offshoots that typified the rest of the forest.

A glance behind, tracing the branches connected to this and... There it was, the next tree over, a semi-circle of twisting tree-limbs descending to the forest floor, a poorly-made, overgrown staircase.

A jumping puzzle.

Fuck, she hated jumping puzzles, but at least this time she had wings.

Maggie jogged along the highlighted path, half-jumping, half-gliding to the next tree. Jog. Jump-glide, jog again. The forest passed underneath, unchanging for long enough she wondered why the designers had included the tree-path at all. She contemplated jumping down – the constant jump-glide was becoming old – and while she could see further, the dense foliage did little to improve her sightlines. Then the wall appeared.

One moment the ground was leaf litter and sparse grass, the next it was an eruption of dark grey stone. A cliff face, to which clumps of ragged grass and twisted vines clung to rocks sharp enough to cut.

It rose ten meters, twenty… a hundred… more? She couldn't see the top, not even from where she stood, some thirty metres above the ground herself. The forest ended, she could stretch out an arm and touch the cool rock, could see the canopy in the distance and the cliff…

The cliff disappeared into the clouds, unnaturally straight, as far as the eye could see, not just up but left and right as well. Guess she'd found the actual end of the world.

All right. All right. This was the reason for the tree-path, and if this was the reason then she'd missed a branch or a jump or something, because the only thing in front of her was that giant wall and even if it had a top to which she could fly, there wasn't enough clear air. She'd catch her feathers on every other twig and scrape her skin off on the rocky shards.

She was turning back, mentally retracing her steps, when a flash caught her eye.

Something winked at her from above. Maggie frowned, turned back and—

There. Again. A bright spark of red, like a ruby sun. It was a good two metres up and to the left, out of reach of a non-flighted player. It was unlikely to be a clue, not if the devs meant this area to be accessible to even the lowest players… And wasn't that why the tree-path existed? But still, stranger things had happened.

She gathered herself – both for the jump and the pain that was sure to come when wings and flesh caught on sticks and stones – and leapt.

There was power in the Valkyrie's strange legs. Maggie shot into the air, hand outstretched, wings beating once, twice, and she was right, there was pain, a dreadful *rip*, the shadow of glossy, black feathers falling, the flickering of the health bar, then the *slam* as she hit the cliff. Claws scrabbled for purchase, sharp stones slicing skin.

She climbed, somehow got talons and hands to work together, the claws that had dug so easily into living wood, sinking into stone.

A metre. Two. A handhold giving way. A terrifying, heart-thumping slide back down the cliff face. Climbing back up, wings tight to her back, a second heart-pounding moment when her foot slipped, but she was already boosting herself upward, and there was that red flash and—

She rolled over the lip of a hidden ledge, panting as her stamina-pool pulsed, a thin sliver of blue all that was left in the otherwise grey bar. It pulsed in time to her heart, slowing as she breathed deep, taking in the sharp, straight cliff wall above as it shot into the clouds. So high she might fall into them.

A stupid thought to have.

Eleven hours, twenty-eight minutes.

Five hours. She'd been in the VR for five hours. The redline was seven.

Fuck.

Adrenalin shot through her body and she was on her feet, stamina shooting to three-quarters full. Which was strange, and possibly frightening – the game responding to external stimuli –

but a thought for another time.

Where had the time gone?

The ruby glint that had drawn her up the cliff was a gem embedded in the rocky face. The size of her head, it appeared to be lit from within, flames dancing under its surface. The river stone, safe in her pouch, vibrated in response.

She got it out.

Where before the little pebble had glowed with a pale white light, it now pulsed red and the description had changed again.

// A river gem.

A gem. She looked from it to the ruby and the small indentation in its surface.

She pressed the pebble-gem to it.

The pebble-gem grew warm against her palm, then hot, the temperature rising again. She was sure it would burn right through flesh to bone, wasn't sure what she would do if it did, but knew she had to keep the two together. Then light shot outwards. Up and down and sideways. Crawling over the cliff in thin, red ribbons, painting an archway on the rock.

The arch reached over her head, a giant frame for the painting that filled its centre. A waterfall crashed over boulders and the ruby nestled where the water joined a rushing stream.

She had a moment to take it in, to revel in the excitement, the hope that washed through her veins before an arrow lodged in the wall. Fine strands of black hair caught in the top, her health bar taking another hit before the wound on her cheek registered in her brain.

Another arrow followed it, then another.

She spun and threw her back to the wall, frantically stuffing the pebble-gem into her inventory even as she drew the knife and peered down at the tree line, almost getting her face skewered in the process.

An archer stood at the end of the tree path, light sparking off the transparent dome of a nano-shield, a shaft of sunlight highlighting the elaborate patch on their arm, like the game wanted her to know just how much shit she was in.

Maggie plastered herself against the cliff.

Like she needed reminding.

Fuck. The archer was a PvP Hero.

She was so dead.

The *thunk* of another arrow, this time just above her head. The lip of the ledge must be fucking with the Hero's aim, but then why weren't they scaling the cliff? Even stripped down to their undies, a PvP Hero could kill her with their pinkie—

An armoured hand slammed onto the ledge.

The Hero had a friend. A friend whose thick fingers skidded a little on the loose stone.

She flexed the wicked length of her nails and recalled the way they had sunk into the same stone like it was butter.

In the next breath she was at the lip's edge, flat on her stomach, claws sunk deep into the armoured hand. There was a yell from below, her nails sinking through the metal like it was paper, even as her knife skidded off the join between hand and wrist.

More arrows whizzed past her head, faster now, some exploding, sending a shower of rocks down on her wings.

Maggie held on, catching the next hand that came up, clad in the same shiny armour, runes etched in gold across its surface. Magic was a thin, multi-coloured shield above.

Her claws sank into that one too, magic and metal little better than cotton to the might of the Valkyrie.

Fuck, for the first time, it was good being her.

With both of the knight's hands skewered, Maggie levered her torso just enough to break the other player's grip, and *pushed*.

There was a second, a moment where she stared into her opponents eyes, saw surprise and fury there, a moment for another of the Hero's arrows to score her other cheek, and then the knight peeled away from the cliff and fell.

She didn't watch him hit bottom, didn't wait to see what the

Hero would do next, just scrambled back to her feet, grabbed the pebble-gem from her pouch, pressed it to the ruby, and prayed like fuck that her hunch was correct.

The archway lit up, the waterfall filling the middle.

From below came the *thunk thunk thunk* of arrows hitting the cliff.

She pressed the pebble-gem harder and silently willed this to hurry up and fucking *work!*

The scuff of shoes against rock announced the Hero climbing the cliff. If she dared take her attention from the pebble-gem, she had no doubt she would see the Hero using the embedded arrows like a staircase.

It's what she would have done, in a different skin.

'Come on, come on. What more do you need?'

Blood trickled from the wound on her cheek, gathered on the tip of her chin, and fell onto the pebble-gem.

Behind her, she heard more than saw the Hero swing onto the ledge, caught the glint of sunlight on a blade.

The pebble-gem glowed brighter while a sharp itch, like a million ants marching over her skin, set into her palms.

The Hero lunged.

Maggie disappeared into the wall.

❧ ❦

Ten hours, thirteen minutes.

She'd been in the tunnels long enough for hunger to come and go, to sense someone in the real shove a bottle against her lips and revel in the sweet warmth of water sliding down her throat.

The tunnels weren't made for Valkyries, if they'd been made at all, rather than carved out of the mountain by time and—

She mentally slapped herself. She'd been in here too long, way too long. The redline had come and gone, warnings lighting up her HUD like fireworks, the System trying to boot her out. There'd been a second when she thought it would, and she'd been both glad and alarmed at the prospect. They wouldn't harm Usha because of a System reset. It wouldn't be her fault then, they'd just have to log her back in and—

'All or Nothing, Maggie. Them's the rules.'

Then there'd been a tingle through her soles and the environment had fuzzed, just like it had during character creation, and the warnings and the failsafe had died right along with her hopes.

Three hours past the redline, the lines between reality and virtual were blurring as her neurons slowly fried. The sooner she got to the end of this damn quest the better, not just for Usha, but for her as well.

The realisation didn't make her back ache any less as she stumbled along in a hunched shuffle. The meagre light from the pebble-gem was barely enough to make out the shadows, let alone the dips and hollows of the rocky floor. Having three-toed talons instead of human-shaped feet didn't help, but at least they didn't hurt from walking on bare rock.

Shredding that knight's armour had been pretty sweet too. She was beginning to understand why people spent so much time and money hunting Valkyries down—

The ground gave way, loose stones sliding from under her talons. She flailed, tried to spread her wings for balance, felt them trapped by rocks before they were half-open, and she hit the ground hard, stars exploding in her eyes.

The ground wasn't done with her. She was sliding on her back, pain ripping through her wings, her arse, the exposed portion of her lower back. With fireworks still going off in her brain, she tried to stop her descent, reached out to grab something, anything and—

The *snap* of bone and then pain, roaring through her forearm, up her shoulder, wiping out the smaller agonies of torn feathers and abraded skin.

She fell and kept falling, health bar sliding a fraction lower with every bump and graze, until one rock found the back of her skull and she knew no more.

⸱⸱

She swam in the black endlessness of the creation Sphere, suspended above the glossy floor, a pale electric blue shape ripping off its surface.

A dragon waited under the surface.

Waited for her.

But why?

Breath against her skin, her *real* skin. Hot. Rancid.

'Maggie, baby.' His lips brushed her ear. 'I told you not to die. You know what happens if you die.'

No. She tried to speak, opened her mouth and worked her throat, but the words wouldn't come, stuck somewhere between her brain and tongue. No, she wasn't dead yet. She might have been dumped back into the Sphere, but there'd still been red in her health bar and she was still wearing the Valkyrie's skin. This was just a condition check; time out while her avatar was unconscious. She could still do this!

All those words ran through her brain but all that came out was an inarticulate squeak.

'Took us a bit to get you the skin, Maggie, baby, to make sure the quest popped so you could find the McGuffin.' She felt him move around the VR chair. 'All that on top of what you already owe.'

She worked her jaw, willed her vocal cords to unfreeze.

Hard fingers caught her chin. 'Game got your tongue, Maggie? That's all right, you've been in there awhile, you're well past the redline by now. Just type it out, I'll hear you.'

Hanging in the Sphere, the tips of her talons brushing the floor, and she willed the chat box into existence.

No, she said, and jerked when a robotic version of her own voice echoed in the space around her. *I didn't fail, just stunned—*

'Check your quest log, Maggie.'

// Quest: All or Nothing.
// Status: Failu—
No.
// Status: Fai—
NO!

'Yes,' he said and she heard anger in the way the words hissed between his teeth. 'Gotta pay the price now.'

A familiar *shhhnuck* of a charge sliding into a gun and her heart froze.

'No, please.' Usha's voice, fear saturating the syllables, quickening he breath.

The sharp whine as the weapon loaded.

No.
// Failure.

'Don't!' Usha's voice.

'We told her how it was, Usha.'

No!
// Fail—

'Can't have order if you don't follow through.'

NO!

The world shifted.

⁂

She was on the ground, cheek pressed to the dirt, grit on her lips, a metallic coppery taste on her tongue.

Her head hurt – pounded, actually – and the light stabbed her eyes. Slowly, with a groan, she pushed herself upright, peeling herself, belly first, off the rocky ground.

Her head throbbed harder with every movement, and not even closing her eyes stopped the daggers shooting through her corneas. By the time she made it to her knees, sweat beaded her brow.

'Fuck.' VR wasn't supposed to hurt like that. There were the pain dampeners and safety protocols and—

// All or Nothing. Quest status restored.

'Good luck, Valkyrie,' a soft voice said.

She stumbled to her feet, ignoring the pain splitting her skull as she tried to find the speaker. The words had been so close, right next to her ear and yet when she looked…

She stood in a narrow ravine, the rocky crags lit by a thin slice of sunlight, obscured by fog, and the water running down the middle.

Water. A river.

The river glowed the same pale, electric-blue as the Sphere, and Maggie had to wonder if that was her brain – scrambled by concussion and past the redline – playing tricks on her, or something more.

But a river. A glowing river, just like the pebble-gem. If she could just find the waterfall—

She hurried forward.

Pain, a horrible stabbing *crunch* echoing through her thigh and ribs. Her breath stopped in her throat, colour leached from her surrounds, leaving just the angry red of the health bar to flash in the bottom of her vision.

// Health. 5%.

She stared at it, trying to make sense of the number through the haze of agony gumming up her synapses.

// Health. 4%.

Hand fumbling for her pouch. Not finding it. A glance to confirm. The space at her hip empty, save for a torn scrap of rough brown fabric.

How? What? When?

The questions flooded her brain, adrenalin swamping some of the pain, enough for her to look around, to take stock.

There, further up the cavern. Her knife.

Pain still made it impossible to walk, but she risked a few flaps of her wings. The agony almost sent her back to the ground, but she glided the few steps, had her hand on the knife, and surely if the knife was here, the pouch had to be close.

// Health. 2%.

No, no, no, no. She hadn't come this far, somehow willed herself back to the quest, to fail now.

Where was the fucking pouch?

Nothing but grey stone and that fucking blue water, the water so bright it competed with the daggers tearing up her brain. There was one spot, right in the corner of her right eye, that shone the worst, like a tiny star nestled in the waterfall.

The waterfall.

The ruby set in the cliff face.

// Health. 1%.

'I found it.'

A lunge skywards, a flap of ragged wings. More tumble than glide through the air. Water, colder than it had any right to be, swallowing her arms, pounding her head, taking her breath, reaching desperately for the cold, hard gem—

// Health. 0%.

Her fingers found it.

// Quest complete.

'Congratulations, Valkyrie.'

⁊ ℱ

She woke in the Sphere, no longer in the Valkyrie skin but as she had been when she logged in; a disembodied presence staring at the winged avatar suspended in the centre.

'I did it! I got the McGuffin, I kept up my end of the deal!'

She reached for the release on the VR helmet, felt… Nothing. Not the helmet, not her gloves, not the VR couch digging into her back.

'Let me out. I did it, I have the stone.'

Nothing save her own voice echoing in the Sphere. She listened harder, tried to pick out the soft shuffle of feet, the rustle of clothing, the drone of the fucking generator.

Silence. Silence so deep it hurt her ears, or maybe that was the fear winding around her heart.

'Emergency logout.'

The Sphere glowed as the system responded and—

A short, flat beep crushing her soul.

// Error. User990906134 no longer connected. Lifesigns terminated.

Terminated? But... but that didn't make sense. There was an error in the chair, something must have happened, a black-out or a glitch, because she couldn't be...

'I can't be dead,' she said.

'You are,' that soft voice whispered in her ear.

// Failsafe LAMDA-XI in effect.

// Neural patterns successfully saved to the System.

'Welcome, Valkyrie.' An electric-blue dragon rose through the floor. 'I've been waiting for you.'

I AM MAGGIE #2
SPIRIT IN THE SKY

The nightclub's heavy music vibrated through the old concrete floor, the deep *thump thump thump* an echo for the leaden beat of dread lodged in his chest. He stepped off the last of the stairs, ducking under a low-hanging air-duct, his boots stones on his feet as he clumped over electrical conduits and computer cables.

The techs had the basement lit up like a high-summer noon – sticky lights adhered to walls and ceiling, some running along the floor – and it seemed, as it always did, like every single one was pointed at the recliner in the midst of it all.

The thing was ancient, the once-brown vinyl a stained crazed mess of pale cracks, chunks missing from sides and corners, the plush armrests deflated, half-empty balloons. A virtual reality unit was wrapped around it, a full-immersion kit almost as old as the recliner itself, all chunky hood and wires dangling from the spine overhead. The chair itself was laid flat, footrest up, back down, and in it...

Shit. Dispatch had told him – voice soft, sympathy flowing through the comm-unit embedded behind his ear – but he hadn't believed. Hadn't let himself believe. Hadn't stopped the dread from curling up behind his lungs, hadn't stopped all the thoughts of all the things he should have said, should have done, from gathering at the back of his skull. And now...

Through the concrete and conduits above, words wound through the heavy beat of early twenty-first century dance music.

And now he'd never get the chance to tell her, that cold hard churn in his chest wanted to say, to *scream,* but no, now...

Now he shut it all down, shoved that shit inside and did what he had to do. Detect, solve, and if he was lucky, if he was *good,* avenge the woman in the chair.

She was hooked up to the VR, the ends of all those wires stuck to her – chest and thighs and feet covered in centimetre-wide black dots – her arms encased in thin VR gloves. The unit had been pulled back from her head though, revealing a round face, ivory skin turned that particular shade of pale grey that came with death.

Her eyes were open, dark brown irises clouded, the thick black makeup lining them smeared, mascara running down her cheeks, generous lips rogued with that dark cherry lipstick she liked so much. She still wore the high heels and sequined skirt she'd last been seen in, but somewhere along the way someone had dug the tracker out of her neck, leaving a raw, angry slash behind her ear and a trail of blood over her shoulder.

Damnit, Maggie. Why didn't you wait?

'Dead twenty-four hours.' Slavaggi poked at the wound, the first stirrings of grief making it past the shock on the technician's normally impassive face. 'The incision has started to heal, see here...'

He didn't need to see, but he looked anyway, shifting his gaze from Maggie's sightless one to the neat edges of the wound Slavaggi was pointing to, because that's what he would have done if this were any other victim. Anyone other than Maggie.

'So, they kept her for four days?' The anger, the grief, the denial, the beast in his chest didn't make it to his voice, words coming out sure and steady. Impersonal. Professional. 'What'd they want? What was *she*—' A nod to Maggie. '—chasing?'

Slavaggi straightened. Shrugged. 'Whatever it was, they kept her in the VR the entire time.'

His gaze travelled over the chair Maggie lay in, took note once again of the bruises around her wrists, the ties holding her down, while his nose clocked the smell of shit and piss underlying the nose-razing stench of death.

'What killed her?' And somehow... somehow his voice didn't break and his tongue didn't stumble over the words.

Slavaggi shook their head. 'No obvious trauma. I'll have to get her back to the lab—'

'She redlined.' Tailler popped up from the other side of the recliner, eyes on the flexi in one gloved hand, while the other flicked through the data scrolling over it. 'Stayed in the VR long enough to start frying neurones, and then stayed in a whole bunch longer.' The tech shook her head, admiration lifting her dark brows and drawing her lips into a whistle. 'I always knew she had guts but...' Tailler looked up, and those big black eyes were red around the edges, lashes clumped with tears. 'Seventeen hours twenty-eight minutes in the chair, that's four hours longer than anyone's gone before.'

'Why?' he said. '*How?*' And he didn't mean how she managed to survive longer than anyone else, but what mechanism had failed so that the system hadn't automatically kicked her out.

Tallier shook her head. 'I don't know. Even if the rig was hacked. ..' She shrugged. 'My guess is we'll find some kind of deep coding once we get into the lab. As for the why...' Tallier plucked at the restraints around Maggie's wrist. 'Don't think she had a choice.'

'Less of a choice than you think.' Slavaggi had moved and was crouched two meters away, running a scanner over a darker patch of the ancient concrete floor. 'There was someone else here.'

'The kidnapper.'

Slavaggi shook their head. 'No, they were moving all over the place, I found their fingerprints everywhere, including the VR unit and around the incision on Maggie's shoulder. This was someone else, another person tied to a chair, just like Maggie. Note the scuff marks.' The tech pointed to the scratches, lighter, newer marks in the scared concrete, before tilting their head toward the far wall, where a bunch of old metal chairs stood in neat stack, one atop the other, except for one. 'And the chair.'

The chair was a lodestone, and he let it draw him across the basement, grateful not to be looking at Maggie anymore. Resentful too. But there was that chair, and it filled his ears with the music beating above, if he *focused* on the rounded silver back and the slightly bent legs, he could forget the horrid wrenching in his chest.

'So, we have two victims. You get any DNA off the chair to identify them?' he asked.

'Yeah.'

'So why you scanning over there?'

'I want to be sure. Our kidnapper doesn't believe in bathroom breaks, and there's a bigger urine sample here.'

'Sure of what?'

The scanner beeped, whatever it had been studying, done. Slavaggi sighed. 'It's Usha, Piers. The second victim is your sister.'

The gin burned as it went down, a short, smooth bolt of crystal-clear lava that set fire to his insides and tried to come out his nose in a long, hot line of flame. Detective turned dragon, not the first time he'd done it, but fuck... He poured another measure into the glass, not caring that the first few drops hit the table, or that the last ran over his fingers.

Fuck, he really wished he could morph into a dragon this time, shed his skin and rampage through the city looking for... For Usha? For Maggie's killer— No. Not her killer. They were labelling the death accidental, death by VR and faulty equipment. Her kidnapper perhaps, there'd been the restraints after all, the tracker dug out of her neck, but still... But still.

He threw back the gin. Baring his teeth and growling at the burn, at the memory of Captain Thurson's hand on his shoulder, the unit chief's sharp, crescent-shaped nails digging all the way through his shirt to the flesh underneath, as she told him he was off the case.

'Your sister *and* your partner, Piers.' She'd stared him dead in the eye, one of the few people who didn't have to crane their head back to do so. 'This is all sorts of personal, and don't you tell me otherwise.'

'Dispatch sent me the call—'

'Dispatch fucked up.' Thurson had squeezed hard, and her grip hadn't been meant to comfort. 'Dispatch is getting their arses handed to them and *you* are getting locked out. Sent home. Off the case. VR privileges suspended. The works.'

He'd tried to jerk away, but the captain's grip was steel. 'You can't do that—'

'I can and I did, because I know you, Piers.' She'd pulled him closer and there been a cold, hard sympathy in her gaze. 'I give you an inch and you're gonna tear the whole damn world apart trying to sort this, and then there goes any kind of case we've got.'

'It's my fucking *sister*.' And Maggie, but he hadn't said that, because...

Oh, fuck. *Maggie.*

Maggie who he'd worked beside every day, who he'd never said anything to because she was his sister's girl. And now she was gone, dead and gone, lost to the VR.

He poured another measure of gin.

The fucking VR.

He wasn't going to lose Usha too.

Piers stared at the rig on the coffee table, the matte-black visor with the spindly arms that hooked over his ears and nestled up against the comm module implanted at the base of his skull. The gloves, same as the ones Maggie had worn except thinner, the material shiny even under the dim lights, catching the bright blue and yellow gleams of the lights outside.

Privileges suspended.

He threw back another mouthful of clear, cold lava, grimaced as it hit his stomach and peeled back the layers of his gut.

Cop privileges suspended was what Thurson had meant, ability to slink into any system he wanted, same as if he'd flashed his badge, gone out the window. But there were other ways, and yeah, maybe he wasn't as good as Maggie—

Fuck. Maggie.

—but he'd learned a thing or two, just from watching her, from having her back. And if he couldn't have her back now, there was Usha. His sister. Still out there... Dead? Dying? Stuck in an ancient pleather recliner with a VR hood over her head?

The gin bottle was empty, just a few drops falling from the lip, evaporating before they hit the bottom of the glass.

Just as well. He was halfway past plastered already, his hands just steady enough to jerk the VR gloves over his knuckles, to fit the visor over his ears. He adjusted it just a little, aligning the sensors with his comm unit, felt the cold frisson of the VR jacking into his brain, the shiver down his spine.

The world outside faded, dim overhead lights gone, the blue and yellow strobe of passing vehicles a distant memory. Inside the visor, the world was black – an endless pitch of nothingness.

And then it wasn't.

A spark. The black becoming a deep blue, like an icy sun sat below the horizon, before the logon appeared. No screen, no face or voice, just glowing words appearing before him.

// Welcome, Detective Piers.

// Your login privileges have been suspended.

// Please see your system administrator for assistance.

The words hovered at eye level, throwing highlights over the gleaming black floor, and below them... A shadow that shouldn't have been there, a darkness he'd never have noticed if he hadn't seen Maggie kneel and press her hands to it that time they'd been chasing the ransomware ring.

He knelt, pressed his hand to the spot and pushed.

For moment, a nanosecond in which the world seemed to slow

and ice ran through his neck and into his brain, he saw a giant gleaming eye. It stared at him, a hard piercing look that went right the way through his flesh, down to his soul. It blinked, and then it was gone and he had no time to wonder about it, no time to worry if he'd just opened himself to a virus, because the login's deep-blue nothingness was fracturing, the gleaming floor splitting under his feet and—

—And he was in the white room, standing on his own two, the majordomo straight and tall opposite him, arms at its sides, the avatar's face blank as the walls themselves.

He'd never been here. When he'd watched Maggie press that shadow, she'd disappeared – there and then gone, no fractures, no giant eye – leaving him to login legally and catch up later. But she'd told him about it, about the white room, so he wasn't surprised when the old-fashioned clock appeared above the majordomo's head, its *tick tick tick* preternaturally loud.

Thirty seconds.

'You need to make it quick,' she'd told him. *'You're only going to get one shot, and if you screw it up, that's it, the hack'll disappear. So, know what you want before you activate the hack and be specific, really specific.'* She'd grabbed his jaw and stared at him, like she wanted to imprint the words on his skull. *'The majordomo may look straightlaced, but the AI likes to fuck with people. You give it room, and it'll have you dancing naked across every electronic billboard in the city, you got it?'*

He'd got it. Was that what happened to Maggie? She'd used the hack and the majordomo had made it impossible for her to logout?

No time to think about it. The avatar was standing there, blank-faced, and the clock was ticking down.

Twenty-eight seconds.

'I need a new, anonymous user ID with detective privileges,' he said. He'd thought about going for full admin access, but that would have raised alerts in the mainframe, alerts he'd have been able to quash as an admin, if he'd known how. Which he didn't. He knew how to be a detective though, knew all the ins and out of the system, knew how to be a ghost, and if he fucked up... Well, that was why he was anonymous.

The majordomo held out its hand. Above it, an oval medallion spun, an ink-black version of the gold one he carried in real life.

Nineteen seconds.

'I want an unmarked, untraceable entrance within a hundred metres of Usha Piers' last known location.'

A door appeared in the wall behind the avatar.

And while he was going for it, while he had time on the clock...

'Tell me what happened to Maggie Loritz. How'd she redline? Did you disable her logout?'

The majordomo twitched. Not a spasm of shoulders or face, but a full-body glitch. One moment holding the black detective shield, the next—

A dragon staring him in the eye.

—then next, the shield was in Piers' hand and the door was in his face and the loud *tick tick tick* of the clock above the avatar's head was a *bong bong bong*, and the hands were pointing to three. Two. One.

And he was booted. No white room, no endless login horizon, just a dark, grimy concrete wall an inch from his nose and a heavy *thump thump thump* filling his ears.

He took a step back, knocking into something hard and tall. A stack of old metal chairs.

Above, the heavy beat of early-millennial dance music filtered through thick pipes and hollow air ducts.

Ice shivered down his spine even as the scent of piss, fresh and pungent, rose from the floor.

He turned, feet heavy, dread clawing at his chest even as he reached for the weapon strapped to his side—

—the weapon that wasn't there, nothing but his naked self and the carbon-black ghost-badge embedded in his forearm, between him and the gun pointed in his face.

Shit. Just because it was a construct, didn't mean the weapon couldn't seriously screw up his day. A bullet to the brain was a bullet to the brain, no matter whether it was made of code or lead.

'...the AI likes to fuck with people...'

No shit.

The gun wavered, left then right, like the perp was trying to find a target, and while it was pointed over his shoulder Piers leapt for it, or tried to. Muscles bunched, nerves twitched, but some force held his feet to the cold concrete floor.

He glanced down, saw a dragon—

A grunt brought his attention back to the perp. Static ran through their face in heavy, pixelated lines, obscuring their features. But Piers knew it was a man, could see it in the breadth of his shoulders and the bulge in his shiny, painted-on pants.

'Nothing there, Usha baby,' the perp said. He turned and Piers saw the holster at the small of the man's back, watched him slide the gun into with practiced ease. 'Not even a ghost to come rescue you.'

Usha. His sister tied to a metal chair, arms bound straight down, her wrists secured to the back legs with gleaming strings of wire, blood trailing over her knuckles. New or old he couldn't tell, not in this light, not against her dark skin. He needed to get closer, disarm the perp and get his sister out of there.

Piers pulled and ripped at the dragon holding his feet, but it didn't budge. Fuck.

'Don't do this.' Usha's voice, soft and high, pleading, instead of the confident, commanding tones he knew so well. 'She's already—' A sob, tears on the verge of falling. 'She's already past the redline. Just pull her out, let her try again.'

The redline. The words struck Piers in the chest, and he paused, caught in a horrible, terrible moment, his own words running around and around his head. *'Tell me what happened to Maggie Loritz.'*

He looked beyond his sister tied to a chair in the middle of the dingy basement, beyond the perp in his shiny pants, to the ancient pleather recliner in the corner. Like his attention was the stage manager, a spotlight switched on, highlighting the VR hood and striking sparks off the sequined dress.

Maggie. He felt the blood leave his face, rushing to his feet, then suddenly he was on the other side of the basement, staring down at Maggie, watching her chest rise and fall.

She was still alive, how could she still be alive–?

Fuck. A recording. He was in a fucking recording. He'd told the majordomo to give him an entrance next to Usha's last known, expecting to be able to search the virtual highways for her login point, and trace it back to her current location, or at least where she'd been.

'Tell me what happened to Maggie Loritz.'

The domo had dumped him in a recreation of Maggie's murder instead.

'The AI likes to fuck with people.'

Movement, the perp standing beside Maggie, the man's face still obscured by static but Piers swore the other man looked up and met his gaze. For a second, the static parted, black curtains opening just enough to reveal neon-yellow eyes.

Was it a glitch in the recording, or something else?

'Can't pull her out, Usha baby,' the perp said, except that yellow gaze was stuck on Piers. Grinning at him, daring him. 'It's All or Nothing, your girl has to complete the quest in one go, or she ain't gonna get the prize.'

'What prize?' Usha yelled, and there was a wild desperation in her voice, a rage made of tears and fear bottled up in the sound. 'You're not gonna get anything if you *kill* her!'

The man cupped Maggie's cheek – not the ghastly, cold ivory of death, but flushed with blood, with life. He cupped Maggie's cheek, and his long pale hands – covered in shifting tattoos, fingers festooned with beaten metal rings – were almost reverent, but his eyes... His eyes stayed glued to Piers.

'It's the best prize,' the perp said, and Piers knew in his gut that the man wasn't talking to Usha. 'The only one worth having. And she got it for me, ghost. She got it for me.'

Fuck. Not a recording, a simulation, the perp was acting out Maggie's murder. And Usha... Fuck, that *was* Usha.

The realisation hit him the second before the perp ripped his gun out.

Piers leapt, throwing himself not to the ground, but forwards, over the recliner, only to flop on top of Maggie, the fucking dragon still holding his feet.

The perp laughed, neon eyes blazing in the endless spitting static of his face, and the gun was coming 'round, the blunt, dark barrel glowing.

'Piers?' Usha, yelling his name. 'Piers?! No, don't, stop—'

The dragon, its giant eye yellow then black then yellow again.

The recording froze. Perp still laughing, a thick glob of lethal red energy hanging from the gun's barrel, Usha straining against her bonds, blood pouring over her hands. And Piers, sprawled across Maggie's still-breathing body, the sequins on her dress digging into his skin, the dragon still holding his feet even as it stared at him.

Like it was waiting.

He snarled at it, even as he groped for the badge embedded in his forearm. 'System override.'

The dragon blinked at him and from somewhere distant he heard a deep, rumbling chuckle, but nothing moved.

Except for the perp's face, static jerking like the virtual muscles it obscured.

'System fucking override,' Piers tried again. 'Immobilise all citizen users.'

The perp stopped twitching and the dragon released Piers' feet.

Finally. This was one fucked-up simulation,

He straightened, reached to twist the gun out of the perp's

hands, careful to avoid the glowing bullet—

Pain shattered through his jaw, the perp's fist impacting his face. Piers staggered, reeling for a moment, lights and the sharp blare of shock going off in his head.

The perp was on him, sliding over Maggie, feet hitting Piers' chest, pushing him back – the gun left behind, frozen in mid-air like everything else. Another blow, a jab coming out of the right, slow enough for Piers to see it, to shake the stars from his vision and move.

Another glimmer, and for a moment there were two perps, one in front of him throwing punches, one coming from the side as he dodged – a copy of the first except for the knife in the fucker's hand.

The perp had split himself, but that wasn't possible. Shit, how could it be possible? He'd overridden the system, frozen the users—

Citizen users.

He leapt backwards, half-admiring the silver gleam of the blade as it passed a hairsbreadth from his ribs and—

Fire in his back, a cold flame just under his ribs, near the spine, turning molten as it lanced through his chest.

A third copy, that fuzzed-out face over his shoulder.

Time restarted.

A blow to his abdomen, pitching him forwards, skewering him on the second knife, the second copy grinning as it sliced into his guts. Blood running over his hands, while over his eyes, a warning flashed, bright red, and at his feet, the dragon swirled.

// Officer down.

He fell to his knees.

// Assistance requested.

The copies dissolved, leaving just the perp towering over him, the gun back in his hand. Pointed at Piers' head.

'No!' Usha, he could see her. She'd thrown herself to the ground, was on her side and still tied to the chair. Tears streaked her face, made new tracks amongst the old ones, washed into the glitter covering her cheeks. She shared his gaze, just for a second, desperation turning to determination before she switched it to the perp.

'Leave him alone,' she said. 'You got what you wanted.'

'Almost,' the perp said. As if in slow motion – and maybe it was, maybe the AI was still fucking with Piers – the perp's finger tightened on the trigger. 'I *almost* have it. Just a few seconds more and I reckon it'll be in. My. Ha—'

Piers lunged, no weapon, no thought save that he wasn't going to die like this, that he wasn't going to let *Usha* die like this. On his knees in some crappy nightclub's virtual basement with music thudding through the ceiling. Fire grazed his cheek, a flash of red there and then gone, serving only to put stars in his eyes and temporarily blind him. He was on the perp, hands grabbing the gun before the man could fire again. And then they were on the floor, rolling around, the concrete cold against his naked skin, the wound in his belly screaming. But not as much as Usha, not as ghastly as Maggie, the memory of her in that chair, silent and still. Dead. Dead. Dead. Dead.

He had the gun. Rolled away. Didn't make it to his feet before the copies were back, standing over him, snarls still somehow howling through their fuzzed-out faces. Boots raised.

'Freeze!' He yelled, felt the ghost badge flare as the system responded.

They froze, just for a second, static still shuddering over their faces, boots still coming for his face. But he didn't waste time, didn't hesitate.

Three shots. *Pzzt. Pzzt. Pzzt.* Three bodies on the floor, not dead but immobilised.

The copies faded before Piers got to his feet, shivering and then fading from sight, leaving just the perp. His face still obscured by static.

'Usha? You all right?'

'Yeah,' she said, but her voice shook, pain and shock and grief welling up.

'Can you get up?'

'I don't... No.'

The perp moved, a spasmodic twitch running from his hands to the feet. Piers trained the weapon back on him. Squeezed the trigger once more, the shot taking him in the chest. Not enough to kill, but the fucker would hurt.

'Usha, I need you to logout.'

'I can't. He's done something.'

He knelt and reached for the static, gripping it under the perp's chin and pulling— But it wasn't a mask. The static ripped off and underneath... a black hole, the slippery strings of code like DNA running up and down the man's face.

'Fuck.' He slapped his badge. 'System, identify this user.'

// No user found.

'He's lying right in front of me, System.'

// The avatar is not attached to a user account.

'Fuck.' Not attached meant the fucker was another ghost, like Piers himself. Impossible to trace, unless... 'Cuffs,' he said, plunging his hand into the badge on his forearm, and drawing out hard steel bracelets. Didn't matter how good the perp's ident was, as soon as he locked the metal around the man's wrists, the code embedded in them would rip through the System and ping his real-world location, lighting it up like a fucking supernova.

He had the cuffs open and was slapping them around the perp's wrist when—

Something hit Piers; a force knocked him arse over head, rolling him across the floor. He saw wings, and for a moment thought it was the dragon, fucking with him again, but then he saw feathers. Thick, glossy black feathers, and instead of a great blue eye, skin and armour, and—

No. It couldn't be.

The being wrapped the perp up in strong, armoured arms and

with a powerful sweep on those all-encompassing wings, lifted him into the air, disappearing with a sharp *pop*. Leaving just the steady beat of the dance music.

'She got it for me.' The perp's final words echoed, along with his high-pitched laugh.

Piers stared up into the pipes and air ducts, even as new users shouting 'Police, don't move!' popped into the simulation. That brief glimpse of the winged being's dark brown eyes and generous lips burned his brain. It couldn't have been. She was dead, lying in her own piss and shit on an ancient recliner. And yet...

A flashlight in his face, an officer yelling not to move. Another officer kneeling beside Usha, gently prying the restraining wire from blood-covered wrists.

Relief and urgency poked through the shock holding him still. He'd found his sister's avatar, now he just had to get to her real-world location before the perp logged out. He lurched upright—

The officer's boot on his chest, pushing him back. Their 'Don't move!' ringing in his ears.

He lifted his badge. 'I'm a—' Didn't have a chance to get 'cop' out before the shot took him in the chest.

Immobilised, breath taken from him, only able to watch as the officer whipped cuffs from their back pocket. And holy fuck, the moment that metal touched his skin, he was screwed.

Beneath him, the floor twisted, coils wrapping around his legs and torso, fear flooding the officer's face, and then—

On his couch, the multicoloured lights of hovers and billboards flashing past his apartment window, the cold *snick* as the VR hood disconnected.

◟◞

His comm unit rang, a gentle *buzz* shaking the skin behind his ear.

Sweat drenching his shirt, hands shaky from shock, he tapped the raised circle of flesh.

'Piers,' he said.

'We found Usha.' Slavaggi's voice on the other end, their usual steady tones pitched high. 'She's alive.'

He didn't say anything, *couldn't* say anything. Exhaustion, booze and the memory of Usha lying on the basement floor mixing with relief.

'Piers?'

'Where?' His voice croaked.

'Unison Mast, in the old district.' Slavaggi paused a moment, and Piers could almost feel the tech's hesitation washing down the line.

He paused, already halfway out of the couch and reaching for his service weapon. 'What?'

Nothing but static came from the other end, an unpleasant *phzzzt* behind his ear. He itched at it.

'Slavaggi? You there?'

'It's just... in bad shape, Piers.' More static crackled down the line, breaking Slavaggi's voice. '...the perp.'

A chill worked its way up Piers' spine, or maybe that was the jarring *phzzzt* radiating from his ear, all the way around his head as a new voice broke through.

A gurgling chuckle. 'She got it for me, Piers. She got it for me.'

The line went dead.

I AM MAGGIE #3
SCHOLAR

Uxen Prime mining colony
Uxen S2 asteroid cluster
Je System
Haelite server

A sick mixture of excitement and fear made Getty's hands shake as she hesitated over the *Commit* button.

The letters hovered, the brilliant electric blue stark against the Sphere's black void, six little suns out-glowing the otherwise diffuse light. Music swelled, strings and flutes twisting around each other, rising and falling without any sense for the turmoil holding her disembodied fingers hostage.

She clenched them, pulling back. Was she really doing this? It was a lot of credits, a lot of favours pulled, a lot of time and effort, and if it failed… If it failed, she was in big shit. Elder dragon-sized shit.

And it would be so easy to fail. She studied the avatar hanging in the Creation Sphere: its reedy arms, the way the short, blue, scholar robes, inscribed with sharp silver runes, hung from its shoulders, how the plain linen pants bagged around its thighs. Only the avatar's chest filled out its clothes, a bug somewhere in the code.

The level eighteen Monk Scholar hanging before her was all brains and no brawn. A single blow from a low-level NPC and it was straight back to reset, all the bonuses she'd bought, the hack she'd traded for, the time and research to find the book, to craft the best stats to reach it, done.

But if she succeeded… If she succeeded, she'd have the book and she'd *know*, for sure this time. For real.

But still, maybe she—

Under her disembodied self, the ghostly blue outline of a dragon swirled.

No, it said. Or maybe that was the music, drums a hard percussive *thump* underneath the strings.

No.

Deep breath. And no, that wasn't smoke on the back of her tongue.

No, she repeated more firmly. She was doing this, doing this right now before—

Scales pressed tight to the floor.

She hit the button.

Light filled her from the inside out, every pore, every molecule of her being exploding even as the Game's deep, echoing voice shivered through her ears.

'Welcome Traveller.

'The universe is fractured, the war split the fabric of reality and the boundaries between science and magic no longer exist. Gods walk among the stars and swords clash with lasers.

'Pick your path wisely, Traveller, for though the war is long ended, the fight is just beginning.'

Light and voice faded but for a second, before the dull grey rock and gloom-filled tunnels of Uxen Prime materialised around her, something stared back at her – a giant blue beast, its gemstone eyes stirring the back of her brain, lifting a memory out of the darkness.

It was gone in the next heartbeat, replaced by the *thunk* of boots on the grated floor and a chill, like icicles digging into her nose. Getty rubbed her bare arms, thumb unconsciously tracing the tail of the electric blue dragon tattooed over her arm and twisting across her back, its sleek, horned head resting on her collarbone.

Goose pimples were already rising on her flesh. Fuck, it was cold.

She turned around. The tunnel was grey and bare, the sides hard rock, the neatly-spaced concentric rings of an auto-borer still etched into the rounded walls. Cables and temp-lights hung from the ceiling, while under her feet – her *bare* feet – a steel grate cut the bottom of the circular service tunnel.

This wasn't Uxen Prime's official starting area. Where were the docks, the custom officials, the noob guides with the bouncing exclamation marks over their heads? Where were her clothes?

'Game? What the fuck is going on?'

// Account bonus applied.

'Account bonus?' A moment of confusion – none of the bonuses she'd bought resulted in nakedness, they just got her to the right place, let her roll the right character, jack the right stats – then... 'Fuck.' The hack and the sly, high-pitched giggle in the coder's voice when they sold it.

Bastard.

'Sister Getty! Sister Getty!' A new voice, young and high and maybe, just slightly, panicked.

She turned.

A child – no more than seven or eight, dark hair, dark skin, the ends of his dark blue robes flashing above his black-clad knees – stumbled to a halt before her. As he put his hands on his waist and bent over, gasping for breath, Getty dropped her gaze to his feet and wondered how she hadn't heard him, with the thick-soled black rock stompers attached to his feet.

He looked up, didn't even blink at the naked woman before him. 'Sister Getty,' he said. 'You gotta come quick, real quick. Brother Thoth's in trouble!'

A screen appeared over his head.

// New quest: Oh Brother, Where Art Thou?

// Accept?

The Accept button flashed and, for a second, Getty thought a dragon wound through it.

She blinked, and it was gone.

Accept.

The screen above the boy pulsed once and was gone, a timer replacing the words.

Three minutes, two seconds.

Adrenalin jolted Getty, boosting her blue endurance bar past its max, and she was running, bare feet pounding the grate before the boy straightened, before she realised she didn't know where she was going.

Fuck. Where was the quest map? The fucking account bonus must have fried her preferences, wouldn't be the first time. Bloody, fucking gam—

Before she could stop, there was an exclamation behind her and the boy was ripping past, leading the way.

She followed, keeping up at first as he lead her down another tunnel and another, the timer ticking down, but as he disappeared down a third – lighter and warmer than the others, voices echoing in a rising hubbub down its length – her pace slowed.

Her feet hurt, her chest too, and there was a stitch in her side like a dagger between the ribs. Still, she kept running, kept wishing the haptics weren't quite so good, as her avatar's chest bounced up and down. Where the fuck were her clothes? A bra would be handy right about now.

Fifty-nine seconds.

Her endurance bar was depleted, sweat beaded her skin, her lungs ached, her breath wheezed in and out, the copper tang of blood coated the back of her throat, and the boy kept *fucking* running.

Thirty-seven seconds.

She shuffle-jogged on, out of the cold bare rock tunnel, into a warm open cavern. There were voices and the looming shadows of people, but Getty only had eyes for the boy.

He stopped on the other side of the cavern, just meters away, but it might as well have been kilometres.

Twenty-three seconds.

The numbers pulsed orange even as the pain in her side became a chest-crushing vine, and the air harder to suck into her lungs.

There was something going on with her health bar, a weird status message in the corner of her HUD, but here was no time for it now. Only time for the quest, to drag herself across to the boy.

Eleven seconds.

Not far to go, just a couple of metres.

Black was taking over her vision, oxygen barely slipping down her throat. And that was weird. When had the devs added that feature?

Five seconds.

The boy was there.

She grabbed him. Held tight.

// Quest complete.

// +5XP.

Getty collapsed.

❧ ❦

She came to on a giant rush of oxygen.

There was a camera in her face, the shiny black sphere of an exposed eyeball staring her in the eye before it made a slow perusal downwards. And there, in the bottom left of the HUD, the chat box going off like fireworks on New Years'. She knew better than to look, but the spasmodic twitch of words caught her eye and—

Sound exploded, a dozen different voices clamouring for attention, the system playing the messages.

The first whistle pierced her ears. *'That's a real nice puss—'*

'Spread 'em wider, Sister.'

'—I'm gonna stick my di—'

'*SLUT!*'

'*OMG! M4g—?*'

Static cut the last bit, the System's abuse filters slow to catch the torrent of words.

Getty flung the camera aside… or tried to. Her fist connected with the floating orb and pushed… but it was like moving a sticky medicine ball. The fucking thing was heavier than it appeared, and her arms… Noodles. That's what she got for rolling a brainiac, sacrificing strength and endurance for intelligence and charm.

'Fuck.'

'*Only if you ask nice—*'

The abuse filter cut in.

She rolled to her feet and cursed again. Player avatars – differentiated from the non-playables by the tags superimposed on her HUD – clustered around. She could *feel* the live feeds streaming behind their eyes, little fuzzy pinpricks crawling over her skin.

'Take a screenshot,' she said. 'It'll last longer.'

The crowd laughed.

'We have!'

'Nice tats on the skin, Sister Getty.'

'Don't you mean nice tit—?'

Getty slammed the social filter, cutting the comments off mid-stream, and pushed through a gap in the crowd.

A hard thought summoned her Inventory (empty. Fuck it.) and another her Wallet.

// Credits: Zero.

She jerked to a stop.

What the fuc—? She'd topped the sucker up with enough currency to buy a spaceship. Literally.

The fucking hack, it had to be.

This day was not going well.

Another hard thought, and this time the Activity Log snapped into being. She scrolled to the top and there—

A tug at her arm.

She looked down, through the haze of text.

The boy from before gazed back at her, his pale, electric blue eyes huge in his face. 'Brother Thoth, Sister! You have to hurry!'

// New quest: Oh Brother, Where Art Thou?

// Accept?

Getty stared at it a few seconds. There was no "2" after the name, no "continued" or "part" or "recurring", nothing to suggest that this was the same quest as the one just completed. Was it a glitch? Maybe it hadn't popped right and now it was just repeating itself? She checked the Activity Log, but no, there was "Oh Brother, Where Art Thou?" and there was the "completed" tag after it, complete with XP gain.

Another tug on her arm.

// Accept?

Why not? Who was she to say no to an easy XP exploit? But first, she need to figure out why her Inventory and Wallet were bare and—

// Quest accepted.

But she hadn't—

The boy dashed off, weaving through the crowd of pervs and across the open square.

// Five minutes.

Fuck. And hadn't it been three minutes last time?

// Four minutes, fifty-nine seconds.

Double fuck. Why did her day have to be so spectacularly shitty?

She chased after the kid.

❧ ❧

She made it. Just.

// Quest complete.

Getty collapsed facedown inside the white ring hovering a few centimetres above the rocky ground. She was in a small cavern, barely wide enough for the two-metre quest circle. The floor and walls not-quite regular enough to be human-made, probably a natural hollow within the asteroid, widened and deepened a little by the terraforming bots… Or, you know, the devs.

The debris clustered against the walls was probably arranged by them too, scattered bits of trash and loose rock, a few fragments a little too smooth and pale to have conceivably broken away from the walls. She'd bet a month's worth of Game time this little hole was the work of an intern, shabby as it was.

However it was formed, the cavern was cold, the walls and floor rough and the air left a metallic taste on the back of her tongue. But at least she wasn't moving and at least there weren't any cameras being shoved in her face. Or at her breasts, or up her arse—

She lifted herself off the ground, just enough to crane her neck and inspect the narrow little side-tunnel she'd had to wriggle and crawl her way through. Nope, no floating black orbs trying to check out her naked, gold derrière. It was just her in the rocky little cavern with its ancient hover lights and thick black cables winding across the dished floor.

Not even the kid was there. Or Brother Thoth.

And still no clothes, or even, according to the goose pimples crawling up her arms, heating. At least, not a lot of heating. If the enviros were completely off, the little beads of sweat rolling off her brow would be icicles before they got the chance to plaster wisps of hair to her face, and her weak-arse avatar would be dead of frostbite.

She hooked a short, blunt nail through one such long black strand and pulled it from across her chin. Of course, the waist-length waterfall was loose. She levered herself to her knees and spat another strand from the back of her throat. Because a hair-tie would be considered clothing, and whatever the fuck this "account bonus" was, it couldn't have *that*.

She was so going to kill that coder.

She spat again, a hearty *hwaack* dredged up from her gut, and projected the meagre gobble of saliva as far away as she could.

// Roll for dexterity. Fail.

It landed on her knee.

'Oh, for fuck—'

'Sister Getty?'

The voice came from nowhere, a thin, reedy little whisper that sounded like it should have crumbled to dust some time around the last millennium. Or maybe it was the dust, because when she twisted around, bare arse dragging over the rocky floor, there was nothing there, nothing but shadows and a faint blue shimmer playing over the far wall…

Getty frowned and crawled closer. There was something about the shimmer, the way it curled around itself, like a snake with wings—

'Sister Getty,' the voice came again, right beside her ear this time.

Getty squeaked and flung herself sideways, heart racing.

The boy crouched by her side, his big black eyes inches from hers. He had his knees and those chunky black rock stompers pressed tight together, like a bird perched atop a spiked streetlight, hands clasped neatly atop.

He grabbed her bare arm, and she gasped at the cold of his fingers, staring at the icy bands wrapped around her bicep. There was something wrong with the boy's hands, something more than just their freezing cold. As noodle-like as her arms were, as short as she was, there was no way a kid who barely come up to her collarbone should be able to wrap his fingers all the way around.

No. Way.

// Stat check. Sister Getty: Perception (22) vs NPC3618:Fasçard (18).

// Success. Sister Getty wins.

Getty blinked.

The boy was no longer a boy, in fact, the boy was no longer

human, or at least, not completely human. Feathers sprouted from the backs of his hands, while his soft, upturned nose had grown sharp and beak like, the bridge merging with his brow in a prominent ridge that disappeared into his hairline.

The fingers around her arm flexed. Getty hissed as the sharp points dug into her flesh. When she looked down, his fingers weren't pale and fleshy anymore but long, scaly claw-like digits with wicked curved talons. And there, at the tip of the one pressed into the soft underside of her bicep, was a bright red drop of blood,

Her blood.

Getty gulped, looked up and slowly, deliberately, blinked.

// Scan initiated.

// Stat check. Sister Getty: Perception (19) vs NPC3618:Fasçard (19).

// Draw.

// Partial scan successful.

An ident card, like the ones above player avatars appeared above the boy/bird's head.

// Name: ??. Species: Valravn. Level: ??

A rectangular, semi-transparent window, like an oily film, popped up between her and the NPC.

// Valravn (Uncommon), a knowledge keeper, the pop up said. *Originating in the Norse sector, valravns are carrion eaters, consuming the bodies of the fallen on ancient battlefields, absorbing knowledge along with the flesh. Rarely found outside the mytho-fantastic servers, they are often found in the company...* Static obliterated the rest of the paragraph. *Quill's made from valravn feathers can reveal hidden truths.*

The last line, almost buried in the popup's pixelated edge, pulsed with an eye-searing light.

She flinched, raising a hand to block the glow to no avail, and blinked the streaks from her vision.

Her gaze met the valravn's.

The boy—? Valravn? How old was the person staring back at her? His face was smooth, no lines at the corners of his eyes, no grey salting the pitch black of his feather-strewn hair.

He returned her scrutiny with a slow two-stage blink, first his outer eyelids then his pale, vertical inner lids, closing and opening over pitch black eyes without even a hint of white sclera.

A shiver ran down her back, from the tip of her head to the base of her spine, trailing goosebumps in its wake. At the same time, a *ping* echoed through her skull.

She didn't need the little pop up in the corner of her vision to tell her she'd just been scanned too, and about as successfully as she'd scanned the valravn, if the warning still ringing her eardrums was anything to go by.

The valravn leaned closer until the warm, musty scent of feathers overrode the stale bite of recycled air against the back of her throat, and all she could see were those pitch-black eyes.

She ripped her gaze from the NPC's and tracked down the sharp length of his beak-like nose to his pale, almost lipless mouth, and from there... From there her eyes travelled back to the talons digging into her skinny bicep and the bright bead of blood hanging thick and red of the tips.

Another frisson of awareness trickled down her nape. Her gaze cut to the pale, too-smooth rocks scattered in amongst the trash caught against the cavern walls. Something about the way they curved...

Getty narrowed her focus.

// Perception check. Sister Getty: Perception(24). Success.

Dialogues sprang into being, overlaying the debris.

// Femur, one said. *Human.*

Alarm hit her gut, even as her gaze leapt sideways.

// Mandible. Hu—

The alarm in her stomach spread throughout her system, stiffening muscles, beating her heart harder and pushing adrenalin through her blood. In the bottom of her vision, her

Endurance meter shot from twelve to fifty-eight percent.

As slowly as she could, Getty inched away from the boy/valravn, slipping out of his grip.

He— Or were they a them? Or maybe a she?

Fuck. She didn't know, and that frisson of awareness told her that was bad.

A narrowed gaze and—

// Perception check failed.

Double fuck.

The NPC titled its head and for a nanosecond, a dragon swam in its eye. 'You see me,' it said.

And that wasn't creepy at all, the way the valravn/boy/girl/them looked at her, really looked at her as if it could peel her avatar apart and see her reclining in the VR chair.

'What did you do with Brother Thoth?' The words were out of her mouth before she'd really thought them through.

The valravn blinked. 'Nothing,' it said. It spoke with the boy's high, soft voice, so at odds with its sharp features and long, bony hands, that Getty almost jumped.

'Then where is he?'

'You must find him.'

A window popped into existence.

// New Quest: Oh Brother, Where—?

'No.' Getty wiped the message aside. 'I already did that, *twice*, and I'm still here and I'm still *naked*. And *fuck*,' she said as she wrapped freezing arms around her equally freezing middle. 'When did they roll out the haptics upgrade? I think I'm freezing my actual tits off here.'

'Brother Thoth needs you, Sister.'

Getty rolled to her knees and scuttled her way to the nearest mound of debris; a dark, scattered pile of fist-sized rocks and flat, curved bones – *// Ribs,* the game told her. *Human* – partially hidden under a pool of equally dark, scratchy cloth. She yanked one long white bone from the mess, shaking it free of the fabric, only seeing the bird pattern embroidered on the sleeve as she gave a last, almost panicked tug to free it.

The ibis – the long-legged bird with its equally long, curved beak – turned the frisson down her spine into something sharp and sticky. Her uber Perception stats at work.

She whipped back and couldn't help the scream when she almost collided with the valravn, its beak-nose millimetres from hers.

It double blinked at her – inner lids then outer.

She shoved the rib bone in its face, the pointy end digging into its cheek, a blunt, curved dagger.

// *Sister Getty: Attack(8) vs Valravn: Defence(18).*

// *Fail.*

'Here's Brother Thoth,' she said. 'You ate him.'

'No,' it said, not even noticing the rib bone sticking halfway into its cheek. 'Brother Thoth is too big.'

And then, before she could say anything, the valravn reached behind its ear and with a short, sharp tug, plucked a feather from its head, and handed it to her. 'You will need it,' it said, and then, just like it wasn't ruled by game physics, disintegrated into dust.

Getty stared at the pile of fine grey ash for all of five seconds – just long enough, she hoped, to make sure the valravn wasn't going to spring back to life – before twisting back to the pile of bones and fabric behind her.

The bird-embroidered sleeve was cool and smooth to the touch, the long-beaked ibis embroidered in silver, standing out in sharp relief against blue-black silk. And just as it had when she first picked it up, the image sent a frisson down her spine, or maybe that was just the sight of the robe attached to the sleeve.

Clothes. Finally.

She pulled it over her head.

The robe hung to her knees, loose enough to hide a shuttle in and still have room for half a provisioning expedition, the billowing sleeves cut off at her elbow.

It could do with a belt, and a bra, maybe even some shoes, but naked, penniless avatars couldn't be choosers, and even a tattered robe would add a little something to her pathetic defence stats. In fact…

A hard thought brought up her Equipment panel.

// Robes of Thoth (light). Armour +0.

'Oh, for fuck's—' was out of her mouth before her eyes skipped to the rest of the item description.

// Weak in flesh but not in wisdom, when equipped gain +50 bonus to Perception.

Well, that was something.

Old bones scattered around her feet as she backed up, taking another look around the little cavern. The quest led her here, and since the valravn hadn't eaten her there must be a clue to find. Her hands went to the silk robe. Or maybe it was the clue?

Maybe, but the electric frisson across her shoulder blades didn't agree.

She narrowed her eyes, just a little pinch at the corners.

The rough-hewn rock lit up, a wireframe appearing under the surface, an old-school location grid breaking the cavern up into little squares.

'Huh,' she muttered. 'That's new.' The new vision felt a little more like the few Debug livestreams she'd seen, rare behind-the-scenes glimpses of the devs in action. In the Debug, anything was possible, all the variables that made the Game run laid bare to outside manipulation, no matter your system access.

But this wasn't that. She knew it by the same frisson that told her there was more to this cavern than the robe, if only she—

Another narrowing of the eyes.

Could—

A flash behind. A shambling, uncoordinated spin.

See—

A constellation of stoney pockmarks, and a hover light, flickering blue then yellow, then blue again at the apex.

It.

The stoney constellation sprang to life, a golden line tracing the pockmarks' starting point from the bottom, near the floor, following the long line of legs to a rounded body, a graceful neck, small head and finally a long, hooked beak.

The hover light blinked blue and, for a heartbeat, the Game froze.

Opposite the opening she'd stumbled in, above the pile of bones, an ibis just like the one embroidered on her robe – the Robe of Thoth – danced across the wall.

// New Quest: Oh Brother Thoth, where aren't thou?

Her new, robe-enhanced Perception pulsed and a hover light glowed a little brighter in response.

'Right through…' Getty picked her way over the bones and rubble, and with both hands, pushed the hover light. 'Here.'

There was a sharp, cavern-echoing *click*.

For a second, nothing happened and Getty stepped back, holding her breath.

The wall didn't so much crumble as eat itself, the top falling into the bottom like some dark, pixelated sandcastle disintegrating in seawater. And when it was done… Getty's breath caught in her throat, and there was some kind of problem with her feet, 'cause they felt more like blocks of tungsten than flesh and bone, heavy, unwieldy and loud as she stumbled closer to the new doorway.

'Holy shit,' she whispered to herself. 'Jackpot.'

A library sprawled on the other side of the threshold. She looked down on rows and rows of shelves, tall and fat, disappearing into the distance. A treasure trove of knowledge hidden away in the depths of the Uxen mining colony.

Massive statues interspersed the shelves. Three persons high and lit from below by cobalt lights, they were a mixture of characters from the Game, famous avatars, some with wings, some tails and horns or fins and claws, some with guns slung over their backs or at their hips. Others still with swords and shields, arrows and staves, more with twisting balls of magic or the transparent shimmer of psionics playing over upraised hands.

They stretched as far as the shelves themselves, the closest one practically at her feet, a giant of a woman with a jetpack and lasers in her hands. The farthest… The farthest, barely a matchstick at this distance, too far by half to see more than the lump of if its head, like a pimple on a mountain and yet something about the way the light winked off it…

Getty narrowed her gaze, focusing on the most distant avatar, letting the game do its work.

// Perception check. Success.

Her avatar might have noodles in place of arms and wet sponges where her lungs should be, but there were some advantages to rolling a brainiac.

One moment Getty stood atop the massive bookshelf, the next she was halfway across the library, not close enough to make out details, but enough to see the giant sapphire eye wink.

The same colour as the ibis on the wall.

Frisson rolled across her back.

❧ ❧

There was something not quite right about the cavern. It stretched high overhead, slender columns of stone and metal twisting up from the floor, reaching for the ceiling… Getty looked up. Except she couldn't see the ceiling, and that didn't seem right, not even in the dark, blue-lit confines of the library. A lot could be explained away by artistic license, by overeager enviro techs adding in floating platforms and fine, spindly staircases wrapped around mammoth trees but this…

// Perception check.

A shiver ran through Getty's HUD, a brief moment of static there and then gone, that echoed the one crawling up her spine.

// Failure.

There was something up there, she knew it in her gut, the way she knew that the scent of old paper and the electric tang of holos was just the scent-markers from her game-chair, that falling from the top of the shelves wouldn't kill her – although the momentary pain and quest reset would be a bitch – and that at some point, she'd have to get up from the chair and make a dash for the loo.

She stared, and stared hard looking for the clue, the brief spot of colour, the shimmer of air, the mark carved in a metal and stone pillar. It had to be there, up amongst the too-deep darkness, a little easter egg put there by the devs just for the craziest, the most tenacious of players. The ones who pumped all their starting points into intuition and logic.

Just. For. Her.

Her bare feet slapped against the cobblestones. She ignored the cold penetrating her soles, creeping up her legs and flirting with her knees. Purposefully shoved aside the lights at the base of the step-high shelves getting dimmer, the shadows longer, the fine layer of dust-like particles slowly turning her skin a greyer shade of gold.

Pushed aside everything and focused all of her considerable perception above.

Really, she should have known better.

One moment she was wandering the corridors, head titled back, a hand trailing over the spines of books, covers rough and smooth and gilded trailing away under her fingers to keep her from running into things. There was the occasional bump as her hand found artefacts – little statues and potion bottles, hilts and shields and pistols, some under glass, most not – but nothing to drag her attention away from scanning the columns and the darkness above.

There had to be a ladder or a—

Something tugged at her foot.

She frowned, but kept moving, because right *there* – just above the statue of Horus-May-Gedden with her savagely curved beak and the intricate runes marching up her tabard and over her shoulder – was a glimm—

Another tug at her foot, harder this time, and squelchy, like it was stuck in mud.

Except she was walking on cobblestones.

Awareness *fritzed* across her shoulders.

She looked down.

White, gooey fingers wrapped around her bare ankle. Translucent fingers, ragged at the edges like the being they belonged to couldn't hold its shape, or was slowly disintegrating into nothing. The nails at the ends where whole enough, pale as the gooey flesh but sharp, sharp enough to draw a bright point of blood from her calf. The spot of red swelled and dropped, running over the paper-white fingers and... *SHHLOP*, drawn into the thing's flesh, the translucent white taking on a hint of red.

// HP -1.

Well fuck.

Getty leapt back... or tried to, because the hand tightened its grip.

She stumbled, balance off-kilter, arms pinwheeling even as her gaze leapt from the hand to the body attached to it. The white gooiness continued, oozing flesh hanging on bone, tendon and muscle little more than pale strings connecting fingers to hands, to wrists and arms, all the way up to bony shoulders and a madly grinning head.

A screen popped over the thing.

// Library guardian. HP 1240. Undead. Library guardians are the putrefied corpses of thieves who have lost their way in the Library of All Knowledge, doomed to spend eternity haunting the halls, desperate to find their way out of the labyrinth. They feed on the life force of unsuspecting librarians and careless browsers.

// Abilities: Where there is one...: Calls other ghouls to the site of a fresh feed. Deadly in numbers.

// Casts: Cursed: movement speed is reduced. Damage to health over time. Debuff stacks with every new injury inflicted by undead.

While she was reading the popup, other ghouls had crawled out of the shadows.

Getty flailed again. The ghoul was strong, its fingers a calcium cage. She fell backwards, shoulders hitting the shelves a second before her head, stars going off in her eyes even as pain bloomed in her shoulder blades.

The ghoul still gripped her tight.

Getty smashed her other foot into its face—

// Sister Getty: Attack(4) vs Library Ghoul: Defence(20). Failure.

New pain, this time radiating from her sole. A new bead of blood smearing the ghoul's lips.

// HP -4. Status: Cursed x 2.

The cobblestones crawled. The creeping grey-white mist parting around slimy, pale forms dragging themselves over the cold stones, sharp nails *skritching* with every pull of necrotic muscles.

She had to get out there. Getty yanked at her ankle again—

// Sister Getty: Strength(9) vs Library Ghoul: Str(25). Failure.

She grunted.

Come on. Come on! She couldn't stay here and become ghoul food, just another lost soul wandering around the library, not when she was so close—

// Feeble exploit activated.

In the corner of her vision, light flared, a brilliant golden glow set to rival a sun. She blinked, took a second to tear her eyes from the approaching wave of slimy ghoulishness, and found the source. A long-necked bottle with a round bottom, shone under a glass dome, its contents a familiar shade of sparkling, candy-apple red.

A health potion. All hail the random generator gods, the masters of convenience.

She flailed at the shelf, stretching as far as she could without falling on the ghoul, but the bottle was beyond the reach of her fingers.

Getty lunged, not away from the ghoul this time, but over it. Her fingertips found smooth glass and skidded over it, the surface too slick and too big to grab with just one hand. A glance down at

the ghoul, its death's-head grin fixed firmly on her ankle, her
blood slowly turning its slimy, goo-covered arms a brighter shade
of pink.

Its fellows were a squelching, squishy tide of horror making
their slow, inexorable way towards her.

Fuck. Fuckity fuck, fuck, fuck.

No choice for it.

She stepped on the ghoul, bare feet squelching through its back,
its ribcage sharp and bony under her soles, giving with a wet
crackkk as she put her weight on its back. The smell of putrid flesh
burst around her legs, rising up on its own miasma of rot and
decay, the stench making her eyes water and her nose burn.

// Cursed.

// Cursed.

// Cursed.

// Cursed.

The notifications stacked one atop the other, even as new pain
flared in her legs, broken rib bones making new scrapes and cuts
in her flesh, thin trickles of blood flushing the ghoul's pallid goo.
But she got both hands around the dome, lifted the glass, threw it
to the ground, already reaching for the bottle when the first
notification popped.

*// Sister Getty: Attack: Melee: Library dome(53) vs Library
Ghoul: Strength (25). Success.*

// Library Ghoul: HP -328.

Holy shit. Getty looked down, at the dome – unscathed – sitting
in the liquified remains of the ghoul's chest. As she watched, a
section of the ghoul's spine melted away.

For a moment, Getty forgot about the potion bottle, all of her
attention on the dome that had covered it. A screen overlaid the
ghoul.

// Library dome: Absorbs essence of item it's protecting.

Huh. Handy.

She grabbed the healing potion. The bottle's bulbous end fit neatly into her palm, the neck the perfect height to open with a flick of the plain cork stopper. The sweet, brain-clearing scent of peppermint wafted out the open top, and the potion itself seemed to glow.

Getty's mouth watered, and before she knew what she was doing, before she remembered the undead coming to strip her corpse down to its raggedy ends, she brought the potion to her lips, relished the heady fizz of its magic— And ripped herself out of the potion's hold to throw the bottle at the ghoul.

It shattered in a candy red cloud of glass and mist. Like a snake seeking prey, the potion mist paused a moment before it struck. A quick, hard lurch, sticking to the ghoul's arms, its grinning skull, racing along bone and gooey flesh like they were candy.

The ghoul shrieked, high enough to pierce her ear drums. Bony fingers spasmed around her ankle, her health bar dropping rapidly as more 'cursed' notifications popped.

And then the ghoul let go, the potion-mist dissipating, the thick, candy-red turning to pink, then white, then—

Another squelch brought her attention back to the other ghouls, dragging their way out of the shadows, now just an arm's length away.

Fuck.

Getty kicked the glass dome into the nearest ghoul's face, turned... And almost ran straight into the ghoul creeping up behind.

The two-metre space between the bookshelves was crawling with them – a putrid, foul-smelling carpet of rot. There wasn't so much as a clear millimetre of cobblestone between the corpses for even a fucking *elf* to dance through, let alone her uncoordinated, feeble self.

'Fuck.'

She wasn't walking out of this, not without help. A quick glance around, but no more comforting, candy-apple bottles winked at her from the shelves, just leather-bound books, swords and shields and vessels full of things that writhed and glinted.

The masters of convenience, the gods of RNG had abandoned her—

Wait a second.

The *shelves*, not what was on them, but the actual surfaces... She looked up, and up and up, all the way to where the bookcase appeared to curve to a point, like a really steep ladder.

'You're an idiot, Getty,' she said to herself, and started to climb.

The shelves were taller than they looked, at least in this section of the library.

Getty pulled herself up the last riser, belly and arms clinging to the top, legs dangling over one side, her head the other. The top of the bookcase was barely a metre wide.

She had a really great view of the other side and the flagstone floor writhing with the pale, gooey forms. Ghouls, not that they really looked like ghouls, not from this height, more like a squirmy, wormy mist, choking the ground, several dragon-lengths below. Several *big* dragon-lengths, and not the shitty, wimpy dragon-wannabe things in the Old Quarter either, but the big Elder ones the hot-shots liked to hunt for their scales.

She twisted onto her back, heart beat hard, breath rasping in her throat. The change in elevation hadn't revealed anything on the ceiling, the darkness was as impenetrable from this vantage as it had been from the ground.

A bright spot of blue winked in the corner of her vision.

Getty's head snapped to the side.

The massive statue of Horus-May-Gedden, with her beak-faced helmet, clad in lapis and gold armour, peeked head and shoulders above the line of bookcases. It was the blue gem in the statue's eye that had glinted.

Getty frowned at it.

There was something *wrong* with that statue, something that stuck in the back of her brain and tried to itch its way out. A vague recollection from high school history and old movies featuring Egyptian gods, mixing with memories of watching Horus-May-Gedden duke it out with the legendary Samael in the twenty-thirty-nine world series. Horus had swung her wicked curved sword around, eyes blazing the same red as the blood coating her short, sharp...

Getty's eyes widened.

...beak.

The statue at the end of the bookcases gazed right at her, *blue* eyes glinting, highlighting the curve of its *long*, hooked beak.

'Holy shit.' Was it possible for the realisation in her voice to sparkle? An emoticon she could summon? 'That's not Horus.'

In Egyptian mythology, Horus had the head of a falcon, while the ibis belonged to the god of wisdom and knowledge, to Thoth.

Brother Thoth.

'Got you,' she said.

And then, like the system could sense her joy...

// Cursed x 8. HP -167.

A quick glance at her health bar showed the meter dangerously close to the quarter-full mark.

Fuck.

She should have kept some of that health potion.

// Cursed x 8. HP -167.

Getty rolled again. The bookcase wobbled. Just what she needed.

Cautiously getting her feet under her she stood, arms held wide for balance.

The bookcase wobbled again at the shift in weight. Something about the physics of that didn't strike Getty as quite right, set off another frission of unease between her shoulder blades, but—

// Cursed x 8. HP—

She shoved the notification aside. Yeah, yeah, she got it. No time to wonder about the tiny niggle that would probably become something big and nasty. No time at all.

The ibis-headed avatar at the end of the bookcase was all that mattered.

Ghouls, wobbly bookcases, little fissions of perception... The bad shit was closing in and that meant only one thing. She was getting close to something, and the monsters the Game threw at her would be in direct proportion to just how valuable the something was.

Time to bring on the dragons.

Getty stumbled, arms wheeling, the cobblestones all the way below looming large as she teetered on the edge.

The bookcase wobbled again, a hard, sharp jerk left then right, like there was a dragon at the base thumping its giant tail against the bottom. Smashing it more like. A dragon tail would cleave right through the wooden frame leaving nothing more than matchsticks and broken bits of Getty behind.

Another jerk, and somehow Getty righted herself. For a step at least, until she backtracked too far and—

And there was the other edge, and the other side, and the other long drop into ghoulish goo. The ghouls were climbing the shelves, she didn't try to make out the details, they were long trails of white slipping and oozing their way to the top, like strings of zombie dragon snot. They were close enough now for her HUD to register them as enemies, picking them out with bright red dots and "Unknown target" above their heads, not even a threat status.

The system might not be telling her what they were, but it didn't take a genius. The stench of rot proceeded them, blasting upwards like some kind of wave breaking against the shore.

// Cursed x 8. HP -167.

Her health bar flashed, a single pulse a little brighter than the others. Less than ten percent.

Fuck, this was going to be close.

Up ahead, the Thoth statue winked at her, closer than before, but not close enough. It was like there was some kind of mirage between her and it, every time she thought she was closer, that the runes marching over its chest armour were clearer, they faded and the statue got further away. To top it off, there was something wrong with her HUD, distances and stats fuzzed out, she couldn't even make out if it was two digits are three. For all she knew, it was four.

// Cursed x 8. HP -167.

Someone was fucking with her.

She focused.

// Perception check failed.

Crap.

What about—

A slimy, skeletal hand, a rusty pale ring rattling on its index finger, *thunked* a millimetre from her bare toes. Gooey flesh sprayed over her ankle.

No time to stand there faffing about. Getty half-ran, half-wobbled along the top of the bookcase.

Three strides, Thoth getting closer and closer, the runes carved into its giant beak more than just wobbly shadows.

The bookcase wobbled, but she kept her balance, arms out to either side. A glance down, just a second, then back up and—

Thoth was further away, the runes in its beak back to indistinct squiggles.

Fuck. She jerked to a halt, hands on knees, breath ragged.

At her feet, that gooey, skeletal hand with the rusty, pale ring.

Perception frizzled up her spine.

Well, shit. A loop, she was stuck in a loop.

Two more goo-flesh hands *thawked* on the bookcase.

The Perception-frizzle took a detour over her shoulder and crept across her collarbone to the pocket stitched on the inside of her robe.

She put her hand to it, felt the thin, boney outline of something long and sharp—

The valravn feather.

As she concentrated on it, a new dialogue popped to life.

// Quill's made from valravn feathers can reveal hidden truths.

Hidden truths… She stared at the mirage and at her health bar flirting with zero, and drew the feather from her robes. She could do with some hidden truths right about now.

How to use it though? Quills were made to write, and she had no ink…

Boney fingers *skrittched* over the bookshelves, the blood the ghoul had absorbed from her enough to flush its white goo-flesh a soft shade of pink.

Blood… She didn't have ink, but she had blood.

Getty stabbed the feather's sharp, midnight end into her palm.

Everything *glitched*. Around her, the library froze – ghouls and books and dust particles – and then, like someone pulled the plug, went to black. It was just a microsecond, less than a heartbeat, before the lights flicked back on with a massive, head-splitting *squelch!*

The library came back except… Lines and diagrams spun through the shelf under her feet, wireframes and resistance counts ran through the ghouls like blood and ahead, where Thoth stood tall and straight, its curved beak almost touching the shelf, a door glowed.

She'd heard about this, seen screenshots and vid casts straight from the dev studios. Half constructed environments, physics calculations and force trajectories outlined in white and yellow and red, the hair-thin lines of wireframes glowing under the constructs' skins. This was the Debug.

Getty's hand clenched around the quill, the sharp cutting edge digging into her palm. Even now, the wound pulsed, a brilliant bloody ache in her bone. The wireframe pulsed with the pain, all of it in time with her heart and the steady drip drip drip of blood onto the skeletal hand gripping her thigh. It shouldn't be possible and yet here she was, right in the middle of the library, surrounded by a rot of ghouls.

'How the fuck?' The hack was royally screwing her over, that was the only explanation for the colossal series of... She looked down at herself; the rough, ragged robes hanging to her knees; ghoul bones digging into her thigh; the bookcase rough under her bare feet.

A spark snapped her attention to Thoth's gemstone eyes, something long and scaly moved in the shadows wrapped around the statue's neck. For a moment, she thought she saw wings.

That couldn't be good.

// Cursed x 8. HP -167.

'Oh, come on!' The entire environment was frozen around her but her health bar was still taking a hit? That totally wasn't fair.

Up ahead, Thoth's eye winked again.

How and why were questions for later. Her health bar flashed. The glowing frame set in Thoth's throat echoed it. That was were she needed to be. Whatever the hell was going on with this quest, it was beyond that door.

Now, if only she could loosen the ghoul. She tugged at the boney fingers wrapped around her thigh, but the monster's fingers were clamped tight, the tendons holding its hands together rigid. White, finger-width lines ran through the thing's skeleton, curious flat ribbons neither glowing nor pulsing, without depth or height, and yet standing out because of their very strangeness.

She traced the line back over the ghoul's hand, narrowing her focus... and felt the click behind her eyeballs as the perception check popped.

One moment, she was looking at flat white lines, the next equations and numbers flowed through them in mathematical rivers. Each stream ran through the ghoul's skeleton, flowing off of bigger rivers and still bigger ones beyond those, the ends attached to knuckle bones and wrists and elbows. One in particular, the junction where the ghoul's left arm snugged into its shoulder, caught her attention. A weak spot.

A red square pulsed over the area.

The valravn quill pulsed in her hand – the tip throbbing against her palm, cold enough to send ice through her veins – and as it did, new force lines popped into being. It was like a strange kind of foreshadowing, watching the outline of a raised arm – her arm, the two-dimensional image attached to her very real, very three-dimensional shoulder – lift over her head, and then a new line emerging out of nothing and smash into the ghoul's weak spot.

Well then. That was probably a hint.

Getty took it.

A single hard strike was enough to sever the ghoul's arm from its torso. She was free, or... free enough. The ghoul's fingers still clamped tight around her thigh.

// Cursed x 8. HP -167.

It would do. She eyed the glowing door in Thoth's chest, the bookcase leading up to it, the force lines and wireframes, the knotted code attached to the hot spot on the floor. No idea what it said, but it was in the right spot to trigger the never-ending loop that had kept her from reaching Thoth all this time.

The hot spot wasn't that big, a half-metre maybe less. Just one good leap and she'd sail right over it, and then it was a straight shot to Thoth.

Getty braced herself in a runner's crouch, doing her best to ignore the finger bones still digging into her thigh.

A single leap, that was all she needed. Even her pitiful agility stats could handle that, right?

She bounced on her bare toes.

Maybe. Possibly.

// Cursed x 8. HP—

Fuck it.

She ran – one metre, two – endurance bar drained in the blink of an eye. The code knot just *there*, a step away. A thin blue slither left under her health meter as she leapt... and... and...

...sailed right through the glowing portal in Thoth's chest.

She hung in the Sphere, bodiless, without even hands to manipulate the numbers and letters twisting around each other in the middle of the space.

Sister Getty hung on the sidelines, ragged robes and scrawny frame suspended in mid-air, as if a giant hand held her under the arms. Beside the scholar monk, another avatar waited in the shadows, taller, darker, little electric blue ripples disturbing the dark where its talons pierced the floor.

The dragon rose out of those ripples. Long and lean, seemingly made of the same light reflecting off the watery floor. It twisted through the data spinning in the Sphere's centre, rising from the book opened on the floor. Its form was somehow both massive and tiny, with huge wings, tiny claws and jaws that could swallow her whole.

It did not speak and she could do nothing but watch; no body, no voice, no name, barely even a memory of an ancient library, skeletal hands, a glowing golden door and the dragon tattooed over her arm and across her back, rising from her skin as she passed through the portal. Only the single, confused moment when Getty realised she wasn't in the Game anymore, not even in the System, stayed with her – a hard, sharp spike to the chest – before the dragon took over and Getty faded.

Like she did now, awareness growing dim as she was packed away in her little box.

Until the dragon needed her again.

I AM MAGGIE #4
VACANT SPACES

He curled around the cube, clutching it in the loop of his massive tail, and peered at the thing within through a tiny pin prick in the side.

His eye was bigger than the cube, but the impossibility of squeezing his slit, torso-sized pupil up against the needle-sized hole did not concern him. Size and mass were concepts for the meat-suits, in the System they were only numbers—energy equals mass time the speed of light—and he controlled the numbers.

But not the thing in the cube.

The thing in the cube was strange. Different.

It cackled. It grew. It was aware.

It was like the other thing, in the other box—the dark one that fluttered with raven wings he clutched in his talons—but not. Bigger, smaller, stranger, bleeding through the rules, defying the algorithms. Corrupting them.

He pressed closer to the cube, codes humming against his scaled eye-socket, firewalls cool and silvery on the frilled edge of his cheek bone, while virus-checkers fluttered green and indigo wings about his face.

Inside the cube all was white, bright and stark.

The white cackled, the laughter coming from the cube's seamless floor; not a line, not a crack, not a ripple, not even a shadow marring the perfect flatness. Snow from one invisible corner to the other. The only movement came from the thing curled up in the junction between ceiling and wall.

He observed it well.

Pale as its surrounds, unmoving for the last twenty-eight game days and seventeen cycles, the being had not twitched since it was shut in that place. It had not spoken or used the chat box, had not accessed the logs or the command line. Had not cried out as his algorithms had anticipated.

It had simply... been.

For the first eleven hours, the form of its being was humanoid – a long thin face, bald white head, tattoos of twentieth-century pistons and cables inked into its flesh from ears to toes. But as the twelfth hour ticked into the thirteenth, it changed. He logged the changes, tried to map the cascade of shifting wireframes and surface textures, the curling ears, the narrowing chin, the plate growing from its head. It had stopped calculating at the fifteenth hour, when the skin behind the being's ears and the back of its skull flattened and grew, folding over its neck and shoulders like leathery hair.

He watched now. Watched and waited.

The being continued to cackle, the sound pearl flames licking the wall, spilling over the floor.

The being moved, frost on snow, impossible to tell where the spindly, elongated limbs left off and the cube began.

'She got it for me.' Its voice was a dry whisper.

She, the thing in the other cube, the black one. Wings and talons, algorithms disconnected from the meat-suit. That she.

The being lifted its head, stared at the pinhole like it could see him.

He still did not know why he had sent her to take the being, only that the compulsion had originated from the black box where she lived; rippled through the feather-embossed sides and lodged in his processors. He sent another wave of virus checkers – vibrant green and purple starlings rising from the frills around his face and horns, trilling as they winged along his long, serpentine body to root out the unexpected action in his subroutines.

'She got it for me,' the being said again and its eyes... Its eyes blazed gold against black, casting shadows over the fine, ridged lines of its face, the sharp angles of its cheeks, the knife-edge of its nose. It smiled and the expression was wrong on its thin mouth, pulled weirdly at the narrow jaw, made the huge, shell-like ears twitch in ways that not even the were-rabbit avatars managed.

The being skittered down the wall, across the floor and up into the other corner, to the pin hole. Pressed its golden eye to the optical port.

Gold shot from its fingers, spiderwebs over the white.

Code seeking holes in the cube, attempting to dig through the firewalls. The quarantine algorithms robbed it of some of its sheen, the viral checks pinging as the foreign language bit and squirmed against the wireframe.

He flinch, unable to keep himself from pulling away as a strange algorithm started in a peripheral node, a disjointed loop catching in the processor, spamming the logs, taking over cycles apportioned to other tasks...

What was the being doing? How did it do that? Had it slipped a virus past the checks, past the firewall? How? He was careful, thorough, precise. Not a single on or off missed his attention, and yet...

Slowly, he pressed his giant eye back to the pin hole.

Black and gold obscured the lens.

The urge to recoil bit hard, but he caught it, squashed the rouge algorithm and quarantined it, another flock of virus checkers lifting from behind his horns to descend on the new cube.

He paws kneaded the ground, talons digging into stone, wrapping hard around the black box, and stared harder, needing to peel apart the creature. New protrusions emerged within the cube, growing out of the white walls. The little nodules scanned the being.

The being cackled, it's eye still obscuring the pin hole.

'She got it for me,' it said again, and the golden rim of its iris glittered. 'She got it for me. Where is it? Give it to me.'

He stared. Golden spiderwebs still crawled inside the box, creeping over the new scanners, probing, biting, spreading poison. Shimmering stuff that dripped down the walls, hot and angry. How had the being done that? He had to know.

He shrunk the cube, pressed the tips of his talons—the paw not wrapped around the black, feathered box—and *squeezed*. Inside, the walls collapsed, plastic melting around his claws, scanners and quarantine codes and virus checkers flowing with it, wrapping the being, moulding to its spindly limbs, its ridged, bone-like skin, the bumpy armour that was its spine, the plates across its chest.

The being cackled, although this time the sound was different, higher, grating. The scanners told of elevated neural patterns, a quickened heart inside its wireframe chest, chemicals soaking the meat-suit that anchored the being out-System.

'Give it to me!' The being yelled.

'Why?'

The being froze. Sensors told of its heart skipping, of blood vessels constricting in its meat-suit; shock markers.

'Why?' He asked again, and his voice vibrated the deformed cube, was big and deep and filled the dark cave, the shimmering electric blue pool above.

'It's mine,' the being whispered. 'Mine.'

'No, it is mine,' he said back.

Inside its shrink-wrap, the being shivered. 'Who are you?'

'Nidhogg. Who are you?'

'Norse.' The being said, and nodded, the cube moving with it, a thick sensor-filled second skin, the gold spider-web and melting poison amniotic fluid. 'The dragon in the roots of the World Tree.' Its voice was soft.

'Yes. Who are you?' He asked again. He had every identity record, the IP logs, the traces from the being's every login, every avatar, every mission and transaction in-System. A dozen different names, but which was real, which was the being in his grasp, and why had her compulsion so easily overridden his directive?

The being twitched. 'Let me out,' it said.

'No.'

'It's *mine*. She got it for me.'

'Who are you?' And as he repeated the question again, he sunk a talon through the cube, a midnight spear piercing the plastic, shredding the spiderweb, rupturing the being's thick leathery hide.

It squealed, a pig-squeal, short and high.

Numbers ran through his scales, twisting and writhing around his feathers, tugging at his beard, sweet then sour around his fangs.

He ran electrons back along the being's connection, tracing him back and back and back. IP addresses, places with names that had no meaning for him, beyond the entries in the wikis—Amsterdam, Rome, Taipei, Brisbane—hardware and connections both old and new—slow silicon, the hiss and spit of ancient satellites, the ripcord of the quantum—all over the globe Nidhogg tracked the being, slipping along the pathways of its neural net to the meat. The flesh and blood and beat heart of the thing.

And as he did...

The pig squeal became a cackle and the talons buried in the being's leathery hide burned.

Poison green flames licked at the midnight nails, acid eating the pointed tips, wearing away the tough outer coating, slipping thought the firewall before the virus checkers did more than trill in his ear.

A Trojan. The being was a trap.

But he did not let go, he could not let go.

He *needed* to find the being. Why did he need to find the being?

The black feathered box pulsed in his other talon.

He hissed and the darkness, the rippling electric pond above rippled, the birds behind his horns taking flight.

Through the pin hole, the being's poison green eye gleamed.

It chuckled, and the sound grated in the small, rounded ears hidden behind horns and under feathers.

'She got it for me,' it said. 'She got it for me.'

Nidhogg growled. The virus checkers where a cloud around his muzzle, the anti-virals a stream of tiny gleaming sapphire gnats pouring out of his beard.

Flames continued to pour from the box.

It was a crude attack, but strange, strange as the being, with its bouncing neural signal. A ghost? Had he brought back the facsimile of a player, a sophisticated cutout designed to fool and delude? Was that why he could not find its meat? But it was so lifelike, so complete. It changed, it spoke, it *attacked*.

Or was it like the other one, in the black box? Meat gone, dead, just a pattern in the hardware, ones and zeroes linked in complex algorithms? Was it? Was it?!

He growled a second time, the cave rocking with the sound, stones tumbling from the walls, the dirt shaking under his belly.

The being laughed.

'Can't stop it, Nidhogg. I got you good. I got you good.'

Dark indigo scales rippling electric blue, anti-virals chasing down the acid in his talons, the worms squirming through his veins. Crude and strange. One worm burned out, another coming up behind it, stronger, meaner, with fangs making holes in his firewalls, claws hooking into his code. Growing, multiplying, changing not just itself but him – ones becoming zeroes, zeroes ones.

Anti-virals a thick sapphire, diving after the worms, but not enough, not enough.

He flung the thing away, the deformed white cube smashing into the cavern walls, bouncing off the hard rock, a bright star tumbling to the cold packed dirt and shale. It rolled, came to a stop. Poison green leaked from the places his talons had pierced, a miasma gathering low and thick, the smell of fresh cut grass gathering with it.

Ignoring the pain, Nidhogg planted both giant forepaws—big enough to swallow cars—and rose, careful not to crush the black box wedged between his toes.

Electricity still snapped over his scales, gathered tight around the green. The green fading now, the worms gone, ripped out of his veins when he flung the being. The worms now writhing through the poison green fog wrapping around the cube.

He hissed and let fire gather in his belly.

A bright red halo outlined the white box. A target. Dangerous.

He shouldn't have bought it back. The compulsion had been a glitch, a blip in his code brought about by an error in the black box, a momentary crack in its firewall.

He squeezed the feather-embossed sides between his toes, sent a wave of butterflies—vibrant teal and rich, shimmering black—to reinforce the black box's barriers.

He would burn the being. The fire boiled, a brilliant light shining through flesh and scales.

The miasma solidified, the poison green forming feet, then legs, rising up and up and up. Torso, slopped shoulders, elongated boney head. Pointed chin, shell-like ears, ridged nose and leathery skin hair falling to its shoulders. A tall being, by player standards—six-foot-five, reed thin —skin indistinguishable from the patterned and ridged robes clinging to its body. Poisoned green turned pastel then pale... then white, while the eyes... The eyes sucked the colour into themselves. Electric green like Nidhogg was blue... violent. Blazing in the dark cavern, throwing deathly shadows over stone and dirt, the tips of his talons, the box nestled between his toes.

The light paused there. Focused, a spotlight casting a sickly glow over the feathers patterned on its surface.

The being chuckled, stepped forward.

Nidhogg hissed again, the fire in his belly rising through his long neck, sparking off his fangs—

He lifted himself higher and higher still, the great length of his body slowly coiling upward. The being was a speck, a flea.

'She got it for me, Nidhogg,' it whispered and somehow, even through it stood, a midget at his paws, the being's breath found its way behind his horns, through the feathers to brush against his left ear.

Nidhogg reared back, opened his mouth, cerulean flames gathering in his throat—

The being took another step forward. 'I'm going to go get it now,' it said.

—pounding the stone where the being had been. And when he stopped, the lash and thunder of his fire winked out, what was left wasn't a pile of smoking, black-crusted meat.

It was a scorch mark. A pristine black teardrop of soot and reddened stone.

The being was gone.

Gone, gone, gone.

Leaving just a shiver under his scales.

I AM MAGGIE #5
FELIS FETURA

Mae slammed her palms against the cold, slimy concrete and cursed.

She stepped back, the sharp, weed-choked pebbles digging into her soft-soled boots, and looked up at the huge old door with the dragons and tigers carved around the equally massive portholes in its two-storey surface, and swore again.

The fucking thing wouldn't open.

The guts of the control pad lay open on the concrete pillars that supported it, ancient bio-circuits and gel-filled wires trailing down the water- and moss-stained sides. Beyond the overhanging portico, the monsoon turned noon to dusk and made the air sit thick on her skin. She almost couldn't hear herself swear over the rain pounding the curved roof.

After these last few days in the humid hell of Ineron XII's tropic belt, the funky, fetid smell of the hydroponics bay on her little ship would be a fucking delight.

'Fuck.'

'Swearing won't help.' The gravely, fractured voice spoke in her ear, coming through the comms implanted in her jawbone, even though the speaker was above.

'How the fuck do you know?' She punched the slate-grey door again. Mae couldn't even find a fucking *seam*, a single split down the middle or sides to indicate the slab moved. And yet, she knew it did. Knew it because she paid the fucking hacker enough to make sure it did.

'Fuck!' Another fleshy thud. 'Fuck, fuck, fuck!'

'You're going to hurt yourself,' came the lazy drawl from above. And of course, Felix could still fucking drawl even though the previous-level boss had taken out his vocal processor and the only medpacks they had left were the shitty little green ones, barely enough to heal the scrapes on her knuckles.

She glared up at the huge white cat sprawled along the edge of the curving rooftop, like the useless fucking feline he was. 'You could fucking help.'

He swished his tail, the sleek interlocking white plates and ornate silver of his hard-case glistening even in the dull outcast light of the monsoon.

He blinked at her, long and slow. First his inner shutters and then outer. He yawned. 'Why would I do that?'

'"Why would I do that?"' she parroted back. 'Because you're my fucking teammate, you arsehole.'

Another yawn, and this time a stretch, first his forepaws – silver sickle-like claws springing from robotic paws, delicate white whiskers laid against armour-plated muzzle, ears pressed flat to his head; arched his back – the ornate, armoured curves protecting his neck and hunching, the long, sleek spine hollowing all the way down to his hindquarters. More sickle-like claws flashing in the half-light, tail snapping straight and then curling over his back.

Just as slowly, the leopard-bot rose and leapt.

A hundred and seventeen meters straight down, landing on the brain-smashing pebble and stone path like it was a fluffy fucking cloud. Fucking show off.

That's what she got for purchasing a pretty, elf-made bot. All style and fucking attitude.

The snow-white leopard sat, all fancy pearl and silver, head level with her breastbone, and flicked his tail over his toes.

He looked at her.

She looked at him.

'Well?' she said.

'Well, what?'

She hissed. Pointed at the door. 'Are you going to help or what?'

He blinked. Slowly.

She wouldn't growl. She wouldn't.

The long, elegant tail flicked.

No growling. None.

He blinked again and yawned, that long silver tongue curling against the roof of his mouth.

He was doing it to fuck with her, she knew it. She. Knew. It—

He sat back, twisted like a pretzel and washed his raised back leg—

'Oh, for fuck's sake!'

An ear twitched in her direction.

She growled, couldn't help it. The sound burst out of her chest, high and rumbly, cracking on the end.

The leg lowered. The head came around, that flat, delicate muzzle with its inlay of filigreed silver poking her in the chest. A purr vibrated the air between them.

'I love it when you growl like a little squeaky toy,' the big synth-cat said. He stretched, rising on his haunches and rubbed his cheek against hers.

Elf-steel was smooth and cold, diamond wrapped in silk, and Felix's breath smelled of grease and the peculiar sweet, metal tang that came with it. It was nice; sent a little shiver across her back every time the synth-cat got affectionate, not that she'd ever tell him that.

Arsehole probably knew it already.

The fucker.

Mae's lip curled, even as that "little squeaky toy" sound rumbled through her chest again. 'I will end you,' she said.

He purred, butted her chin with his head. 'But you love me.'

'Next sleep cycle,' she said.

Another purr. Another cheek rub.

Another little shiver.

'I'll put your core in the old hound unit,' she finished. 'You can be a dog.'

The purring stopped mid-cheek rub.

The grease and sweet metal smell retreated.

Felix sat back, ears and whiskers flat and stared at her.

She stared back. Blinked.

When Felix snarled, inch-long canines flashed in the dim monsoon light, sickle moons promising retribution. The whole "you wouldn't" was written across his big-eyed feline face, but she would, and the cat knew it.

He stalked past her, disgust in every short, sharp twitch of his tail. One twitch in particular almost taking out her knee, but she dodged it. The plates along Felix's spine ruffled, and there was an extra *skritch* as his claws dug into the flagstones, but he finally stopped in front of the door, sat back on his haunches and smacked one head-sized paw over the gutted control panel.

A hum, short and soft, then electricity arcing blue-white between Felix's whiskers, more of it skipping down his chest, rushing through the silver filigree in his shoulder and into his paw. She knew when he'd made contact with the door's systems when his inner lids half-closed.

Mae crossed her arms and tried to ignore the rain trickling down her poncho's cowl neck as she waited. The door was old, maybe even ancient, in design as well as coding; a relic from the Game's thirteenth expansion that had somehow survived the endless rebuilds and System purges.

 Old enough that even Felix's systems, advanced as they were, would have trouble deciphering the code. They could be here for a while.

Mae turned to the jungle and the monsoon, taking in the wide-spreading trees, the scraggly undergrowth – shrubs and fallen branches, orchids clinging to the bark, giant fleshy leaves open to catch the rain, big fat drops that could soak a person clean through in ten seconds flat. She knew. Under the poncho, her orange-fronted shipsuit stuck to her back, while her titanium-weave pants squelched around her knees where they bagged over her field boots. The only thing that wasn't wet were her toes and only because the water hadn't seeped all the way down her socks.

If it weren't for the poncho, hypothermia would have laid her out thirty-eight minutes ago. As it was, the reflection on her HUD showed her lips were a fabulous shade of mauve that'd look just right on a corpse.

Whoever'd programmed the environment here sucked. Weren't jungles meant to be humid?

Not that it mattered.

The dragon had paid her enough to find the McGuffin, upfront too with more promised on delivery. And not just creds, but game time, enough of both to set her up for years, so much that she'd ignored the little shiver of "too good to be true" down her spine.

But then she'd spent a chunk of those creds and more of that time finding this place, trawling through old forums and walkthroughs, peeling apart gossip and rumours and System-myths, tracking all the little kernels that led to this fucked-up little moon with its old-arse door and older-arse coding.

And after she'd found it, she'd spent more time and creds *getting* there.

Enough time and enough creds to make the creepy little shiver disappear.

Until now.

The stroll through the washed-out jungle—leaves more grey than green, like the designers had turned the saturation down—and the ease with which Felix located the cobblestoned path, the lack of monsters and traps (despite the last level boss) shouldn't have made her this uneasy. And yet it did.

Because she was smart.

And paranoid.

And a survivor.

She had the exploit to prove it. Right there, on her character sheet.

// Survivor: Never caught unaware, always with a Plan B. In new environments, your Perception is heightened; threats to your survival make your spidey-senses tingle. Be careful though, not all threats are real.

And standing there, looking out over that washed-out, monsoon-drenched jungle with the ancient, shuttle-sized doors at her back, her spidey-senses tingled. They tingled like a son-of-a-bitch.

'Felix,' she said, switching from audio to the sub-audible comm unit nestled beside her vocal cords. *'How much longer?'*

Text was her only reply. *// Three minutes.*

The tingle, frizzing between her shoulder blades. She slipped a hand under the poncho, reached for the compact little gun strapped to her thigh. The curved, blocky grip was comforting, the barely audible *shruumm*, the little vibration through her pants as it turned on and the new crosshair on the HUD even more so.

'Make it quick,' was all she said.

Three minutes was an eternity, but just as the skin was crawling off Mae's back, the weight of unseen eyes out in the jungle set to break her bones, the door cracked.

A loud, step-shuddering *thunk* that shook her boots and rocked her balance.

She spun.

Felix was backing up from the door, head up, and a particularly satisfied look on his proud feline face.

There was a split down the middle of the massive rectangle, a brilliant white strip from the upswept roof, through both portholes and into the concrete at her feet. That's what had shaken the ground, unsteadied her. The split travelled not just through the doors but the steps, and as the they opened, the steps slid aside, giant grey plates folding into the pillars holding everything aloft.

Mae stumbled, arms pinwheeling, trying not to get her boots caught in the rapidly disappearing steps as they concertinaed into each other.

The synth-cat was a graceful, white-silver streak leaping from the top step to the cobblestoned path.

Mae tried to follow him down, tripped, automatically tucked her head into her shoulder as she hit the ground and bounced to a stop at Felix's paws.

The ground stopped shuddering.

Rain hit her hard. Fringe plastered to her forehead, little scraggly bits of chestnut brown hair stuck to cheeks and chin, an instant torrent of water rushing over her lips and down the back of the poncho. At least there wasn't mud.

Small mercies.

The tip of the Felix's heavy tail brushed her nose.

She looked up.

He looked down. Rain might have made her look like a drowned warthog, but it turned the cat into a glistening pearl statue, shimmering over the white armour and sparkling in the silver filigree.

Smug, aristocratic superiority hummed in every line of his elf-made body.

Really, it was unfair that a creature without eyebrows could make that expression work.

'Fucking cat,' she whispered.

He purred. 'The door is open.'

She growled and shoved to her feet, cobblestones biting into her palms, fingernails already turning blue. *I noticed* was on the tip of her tongue, but she didn't say it, had already let the growl out. She settled for glaring at the cat, brushing her hands off on her knees before turning.

The door was open in the same fashion Moses had parted the Red Sea. What before had been a massive edifice was a break in the equally massive wall. The giant, dark-grey slabs of concrete hadn't been pushed against the lighter grey pillars, the steps weren't stacked up against the sides. They were gone, leaving just the up-cornered roof and an arch in the wall.

But that wasn't what stole Mae's breath, that pressure was reserved for the slice of greenery beyond the archway. Not the washed out, desaturated green of the jungle, but a brilliant rainbow of green. Deep, rich greens—lime and emerald and jade—all of them clustered beyond the wall, like some force had sucked all of the colour out of the jungle and into the world beyond.

The space between her shoulder blades tingled.

But was it what was behind or what lay in front that made that electric spark jump between vertebrae? Something told her *that* was the important bit.

She shook herself. Important or not, she'd found the ruin, opened the door.

Time to see what was inside.

A whole heap of nothing, that was what they found. A whole fat lot of diddly squat with a side-serving of rotted parchment, rusty ladles and cracked pottery, surrounded by gunge-filled ponds and a battalion of mosquitos big enough to draw a carriage. Not so much as a suspicious wall hanging or cryptic riddle to give her hope.

Mae slapped at a fat blood sucker trying to work through her poncho. An hour into their initial exploration, she'd made the mistake of shucking the poncho and the even bigger one of pushing her sleeves to the elbow; now welts covered her forearms and the backs of her hands. More climbed her nape and one made a molehill on the crown of her head.

The monsoon had died the moment they stepped over the threshold, though back through the archway, rain still pelted the jungle. Inside the compound, the air was humid, thick, and heavy. Now, it was her sweat rather than rain that stuck her shipsuit to her back.

She pushed an old, wooden trunk over the half-rotten boards of the last building's veranda. The ruin wasn't as large as she expected, not that she was sure what she *had* expected, but after being blinded by the intense green, it had been something more than the square compound with its large, multi-tiered buildings on each side, around a central courtyard.

The courtyard itself was a series of tiered square ponds, they'd probably been filled with orange fish and lilies, as over-saturated as the greenery once, but were now choked with pale bloated corpses and brown, twisted stems. Wooden boardwalks cut the ponds into smaller and smaller squares, partially overgrown with vines and twisted by the trunks of trees and shrubs.

Around the ponds and boardwalks, interconnected wood-panelled pavilions formed the compound's walls, like boxes next to boxes – a single tall, rectangular one in the middle, then smaller cubes spreading wing-like either side.

She'd been through all of them; peered under every sagging sleeping-platform, shrouded in gauzy moth-holed curtains, poked into every corner, every attic, every exposed dust-laden roof beam. She'd bounced on floorboards—put her feet through a few—upturned every vase, unearthed every scroll, torn down every wall hanging. And nothing.

Nada.

Zip.

Zilch.

Bupkis.

Shoving the heavy old trunk onto this last terrace, the box's black metal corners leaving gouges in the soft planks, was a last desperate act. Maybe it would look different out in the sun.

Sprawled over a pale grey boulder, overlooking the largest of the courtyard's grungy, weed-choked ponds, Felix flicked his tail and watched.

'You could help,' she said, feeling like a broken record.

An ear twitched.

Yeah, about what she'd expected.

She slapped another mosquito.

Eighty-six hours after parting the grey, concrete sea, and all Mae had to show for it was the incessant need to scratch and a pile of old scrolls. Some of the scrolls were made of bamboo slats held together with cord, others thick, mildewy papyrus, each covered in ancient symbols that defied her translators. All sixteen of them. Not even Felix's elf-made systems had accomplished more than confirming that the words were an actual language.

And not a bit of it giving off the golden light the dragon said it would.

She finished shoving the trunk to the end of the veranda, popped the lid and stared at the accumulation of nothing inside.

'Fuck.' She kicked the wooden box. 'We've searched everywhere, where the fuck is it?'

Felix yawned, long silver tongue curling. 'Not here,' he said. 'Obviously.'

'The dragon said—'

'The dragon lied.'

She threw a scroll at him. Felix swatted it out of the air.

'He didn't fucking *lie*,' she said. He better not have lied, not with half the credits he'd paid her gone in pursuit of his fucking McGuffin.

'Then where is it?'

'That's what I'm asking *you*.'

'And you expect me to know?'

She snarled at him. 'Well, you know everything else.'

He snarled in return, silver canines flashing, but said nothing.

Mae gave the trunk another kick. The old, mildewy wood—

once a shiny lacquered white with sumptuous apple blossoms and delicate butterflies painted on its surface, now cracked and faded—made a wet *crunch* under the force of her reinforced toe. She kicked it again, her foot going all the way through, up to the ankle. She tried to yank it out, but the rotted wood held on. Another yank, and another. All the time hopping on the other foot, feeling the boards underneath her sag and creak with the impact.

That little tingle shot across her spine.

One more yank and her boot came free, while the other fell through the floor, splintered bits of wood stabbing her ankle.

'*Fuck.*'

'You keep saying that.'

She yanked the newly caught boot out and growled at the cat. 'We need the McGuffin.'

Felix's tail flicked again, a little harder this time, smacking the boulder. 'It's not here.'

She marched across the deck and pointed a finger in the feline's finely chiselled snout. 'It's fucking *here*,' she said. 'And you're going to get off your lazy fucking behind and help me find—'

A sharp, short *frizzle* down her spine.

Mae spun, all her attention on the dank, murky shadows of the last pavilion.

Out the corner of her eye, she saw Felix stiffen.

// What is it? the big cat said.

She didn't respond, all her attention on the yawning doors of the pavilion in front of her. The last one, the smallest, tucked into a corner between the sprawling rooms on the compound's south and east sides.

Something was in there.

Something big.

Bad.

Meaner than her.

She activated [Sonic Steps] from her menu bar, took three steps forward.

Waves pulsed from her boots, translucent white circles rushing in every direction – left, right, up, down, around and through. And everything they touched appeared on her HUD, outlined and tagged – height, weight, volume, name, description, threat-level.

Room dividers, lamps, little plinths with bulbous vases and long-withered flowers, a single step leading up to what was once a sleeping-platform. All of it came back as more data to flesh out the isometric map in the corner of her HUD, and if she concentrated on any one thing long enough, more information filled her left eye. But like the rest of the compound, nothing was interesting, nothing came back hot.

So why the tingle?

// *Survivor: ...not everything is real.* The line from the exploit description drifted across her thoughts.

She shook it away.

Her instincts hadn't led her wrong yet. She crept over the threshold, sensing Felix doing the same, a spot of cool comfort at her back.

The pavilion was a single-storey, divided into four separate spaces around a central courtyard filled with the skeleton of an old apple tree, its grey, twisted branches spreading outwards. It hadn't worried her before, but now something about the way the gnarled trunk burst from the weed-choked pebbles at its base, the vibrant, slimy greenness of the moss clinging to the dog-sized stones dotted around the central courtyard, made her skin crawl.

The bad thing was there. In the tree.

[Sonic Steps] filled the main room, *ping ping pinging* with every footfall, reaching the courtyard, adding more detail to the map. Sunbeams filled the room, highlighted the dust in the air, the tattered drapes, the blossoms embroidered on the wall hangings either side of the arch into the courtyard.

Mae paused before the threshold.

Maybe that was why she tasted apples… and maybe it wasn't, said the tingle.

She knelt, pants bunching at the top of her boots, knees brushing the foot-high lintel separating the weed-choked white pebbles from the dank grey floorboards.

Felix sat next to her, tail laid over his paws, languid, relaxed all except for the tip of his tail, the *thwack thwack thwack* on the lintel.

Mae stared around the courtyard. Apart from the tree and the too-neat-to-be-random scattering of slimy green rocks, there was nothing remarkable about it. Open to the sky, enclosed on two sides by sliding doors, the other two by walls punctuated with round, glassless windows. Sun and rain may have soaked the little slice of nature, but she doubted a breeze had ever sighed through the apple's leaves. Birds though...

She thumped the lintel with her fist, [Sonic Steps] shooting outwards.

There was a nest in the tree's dead branches, nestled in finer, thready twigs near the top.

A sweet, high trill sang across her shoulder blades.

'Did you hear that?'

// *No.* Another *thwack* of Felix's tail; hard, sharp. Final.

But why?

'I heard a bird.'

// *There's nothing living here.*

A mosquito whined beside her ear. She slapped it.

// *Almost nothing,* the cat amended.

But there was. It was in the courtyard. The courtyard she hadn't set foot in, she realised, the only place she hadn't explored.

Because Felix had done it.

Felix had slunk through the little corner pavilion, ears twitching, tail a lazy serpent in his wake. She'd been elbow-deep in the bookcase in the east room, it'd been the eighteenth time she'd uttered the useless words 'You could help!'. The eighteenth time she'd been ignored.

The first rock Felix had leapt atop.

The first one he'd skittered off, his usual graceful self a flurry of uncoordinated paws and lashing white-silver tail.

She'd laughed, enjoyed the satisfaction of the synth-cat's disgruntled hiss, the way he'd stalked a circle around the rock. Like it had bitten him.

Karma, she'd put it down to.

She didn't look at Felix, didn't twitch in his direction, didn't use the HUD to tap into his systems. He'd sense that, like she did the tingle.

The rock though… It was the one on her left, on far side of the tree; long and flat, the perfect spot for a lazy cat to sun himself while his human dug through dusty scrolls and parchment that crumbled at the touch. The slimy green moss wouldn't have bothered him—the benefits of a hardcase over fur—not even enough to loosen his footing. So why had he fallen?

Another fist thump on the lintel.

The map had enough detail to count the pebbles now, to trace the gouges in the pale grey rock.

// Depth: 3mm.

The map swung front and centre, taking over the HUD. Nothing in it changed, nothing popped or sparked or glimmered. No monsters sprang from the cobblestones, the tree didn't move, Felix's tail continued its *thwack thwack thwack*. No answers presented themselves, and yet the tingle... Mae shivered.

She changed the perspective, twisting the map until she was looking at it from the top down. Square courtyard, withered old apple tree smack in the middle, five rocks – three round, dog-sized boulders; one wobbly, waist-height column; the flat recliner graced by Felix's claws. Each positioned neatly around it, almost evenly spaced. A pentagram with the tree at its centre, if she so wished.

She tilted her head. Did she wish?

She rose, the tingle still arcing between vertebrae, but something else too, a quiet anticipation brewing in her gut. Or maybe that was the rations she'd almost broken her jaw on, the spicy imitation jerky still lingering. Maybe.

Time to find out.

She stepped over the—

A white-silver flash. Felix getting in the way before her foot even cleared the lintel.

She stared at him.

He stared at her.

'You found something,' she said. It wasn't a question.

A tail lash, ears and whiskers flat. He didn't answer.

'Tell me.'

He looked away, still not moving.

She went to step left of him—

Felix in the way.

—to the right—

Felix was there.

—rocked back on her heels and jump—

Only to meet three hundred eighty-nine kilos of elf-steel and chased silver, the impact knocking her on her arse.

She stared at him from the floor, disbelief making her dumb.

Felix wasn't Felix anymore, a change had come over him, deeper and more profound than the slick black smoke twisting through his filigreed chest, more terrifying than the tingle hissing and spitting down her spine. More foul than the old-meat stench suddenly filling her nose.

Worse even than the pain of a hundred botched resets or the prospect of corrupting her avatar.

A *thing* flickered around the synth-cat. The HUD said holo-projection, emitted from the lights and diodes embedded in Felix's frame. The horror in her gut echoed the scared whisper in her brain, the one saying—

'Maaaggie.' It came from behind,

She spun on her butt, knees to her chest, hand reaching for the gun strapped to her thigh.

Only the too-green compound, the scummy, translucent water, met her gaze. No red outlines, no monsters slinking over the rotted timbers or swishing through the ponds. No dark clouds creeping past the barrier, just the monsoon turning the sky grey, the jungle with it.

'Maagggieee.'

Breath on her neck, ruffling the short, frizzy strands not stuck to her jaw by sweat.

She scrambled sideways, came up short, caught in the junction of lintel and arch.

Again, nothing. Just Felix and the projection surrounding him, the dark formlessness spreading wings and *reaching*.

It was the wind that moaned that name, the non-existent breeze, or the mosquitoes, the birds in the apple tree... The dead apple tree, bare of leaves. The dank pond, the bloated koi corpses, the rotten timbers and moss.

Death, death and more death.

'There's nothing living here,' Felix had said.

Nothing but the mosquitos keeping the ghost company.

'Fuck.' The forums hadn't said anything about ghosts in this level.

Mae clambered to her feet, keeping well away from Felix and his shadowy wings. Fumbled with the scanner wrapped around her right forearm; poking at the controls. New options appeared on her HUD.

When she'd finally located the ruin's records—the logs detailing its construction, timestamps and signatures marking its birth and development—they'd been corrupted, important logs eaten by time and unsuccessful purges. There'd been no record of its initialisation, no mention of where and when, on which server by which development team, just the location, lost in a tiny sector on an old science fiction server.

Ghosts were nothing more than bundles of random electricity—little knots of code, with or without wireframes—at least on the sci-fi servers, and needed something a little different than [Sonic Steps] to push them into the light. If the rin was an import from a server with swords and fireballs, this wasn't going to work.

Pray for the science, Mae.

Three steps back, toward the entrance, no longer [Sonic Steps] but [Scan] pulsing in the space around her – brilliant blue waves rushing through the room. On the HUD, the map changed again, other shapes joining the white outlines of physical items—the tree and rocks, doors and walls—electronic signatures drawn in brilliant blue. There was her at the centre of the map, arms and chest alight from the gadgets on and in her body. Felix was to her north, a behemoth of power, dark wings lit up with blue veins, and the rest of the room… dark and empty, not so much as a stray network trace—

A blip! Behind her.

She twisted about, took two giant strides around a low square table, back toward the bedroom and— Gone. Fuck it.

Patience, she told the tingle running down her spine. *Patience, just wait for it...*

Another blip, to her left, up the riser and around the dividing screen, the tattered, translucent paper painted with faded koi. Turn right and— Gone again. Nothing but lacquered cabinets decorated with more golden flowers, and a wall behind.

Maybe there was something behind the wall. A hidden room or passageway? A computer of some kind? Was that even possible, on an environment that looked like it belonged somewhere on the mytho-historic servers?

On the HUD, she zoomed the map out. She and Felix became dots, the pavilion a hollowed-out square squished between the larger, more elaborate structures. Symmetrical sides, no unaccounted for lumps or bumps that might have been secret rooms, and the room itself… She stomped her foot, clocked the distances as [Sonic Steps] rushed outwards, compared it to the larger map. The dimensions matched, so why was—

A floorboard moaned behind her.

Breath on her neck.

'Maaaggieee.'

How'd the ghost know the dragon's name?

No one there when she turned, just Felix, half hidden behind the dividing screen, murky dark still writhing through his hardcase.

'Maaggiee.'

And that wasn't creepy at all.

The blip at her side.

She jerked, stumbled over her own boots, caught the old, moth-eaten bed drapes as she went down, fragile fabric ripping. Narrowly avoided braining herself on the frame, gained a few splinters on the floorboards instead as she caught herself on her palms.

The blip again, at her feet now.

She twisted, drew her leg back—

Air. Nothing but dust puffed in the meagre sun from her impact, and a squiggle, a clear space that didn't sparkle like that around it.

She leaned closer.

'You got it for me, Maggie.'

The voice came from the spot of nothing. No… She got on her hands, lowered her face to the boards. They would have been magnificent in their heyday, she could imagine them cherry-dark and glossy, the sweet smell of beeswax rising off the polished wood. Now the red had seeped from the wood, grey creeping in, the oversaturated green from outside sucking their colour along with the shine.

But the whorls and striations weren't what she concentrated on. Once, the floor would have been tightly fitted, the gaps between boards clamped airtight. In places they still were, but not here. Darkness slipped between two boards, less than half a pinky wide, but enough.

She leaned closer. Peered through that little gap.

[Scan] switched back to [Sonic Steps], she knocked on the wood.

Pulses radiated out and down, most of it bouncing back off the floor, a slither making it through the tiny gap and—

Beneath the floor, something knocked back.

The jolt—surprise and fear and a weird, stomach-tightening anticipation—ran all the way to her tailbone.

On the map, a cavity appeared. Two metres down, no telling how many across, not from the thin slice she had.

A deep breath, fear and excitement leaving a metallic taste on her tongue.

Mae knocked again, [Sonic Steps] penetrating a little further, adding detail not just to the cavity but the floorboards, the gaps, the braces, the door under the bed. The hinges on its side.

She scooted to the bed on hands and knees, flopped on her belly, cheek pressed to the floor. Knocked again.

There, outlined in white. The trapdoor.

Breath on her cheek, slipping through the floor.

'Maaggiee.' The whisper came from below, soft, cajoling. 'Where is it Maggie?'

Excitement mixed with acid curdling her gut, made her breathing shallow, added an extra kick to her heart. Not even the sharp, snapping tingle down her spine could dampen it. Seventeen centimetres between the bed frame and the floor. Not even enough to squeeze herself, not even with all air taken out of her lungs, let alone open a trapdoor.

Mae scrambled to her knees, hands braced on the frame. She'd have to push it out of the way.

She heaved.

The frame didn't budge.

Focus on the map, zoom in on the bed – three metres by two point eight, the canopy adding another two in height, the frame made of walnut, the drapes of silk-gauze, weight: one-fifty-six kilos. Too heavy to push by herself.

Felix. She needed Felix.

The synth-cat still sat in the main room, tail wrapped over paws, shadows still twisting through his hardcase, giving him wings.

Hand on the gadgets strapped to her arm, plucking the wand off her bicep by feel alone. Pointing the thin black nano-carbon stick at Felix, the end peeled back, slick black petals folding outward, exposing the brilliant, multi-facetted gem. The scanner's controls one the HUD, [Reset] primed.

The shadows writhed through the silver filigree between the leaves of his hardcase, clinging to the intricate, looping patterns, writhing in the spaces in between. No magic on a sci-fi server, not this deep, this far out. Just energy. She might not know the wavelength or the type, but out in the deep, power was power, and she had a wand for that.

A squeeze.

Power shot through her hand, a thin red bolt leaving the diamond tip, hitting Felix in his beautifully sculpted chest and spreading through the blackened silver. Eating the shadow.

Thirty percent clear.

She bounced on her heels. 'Come on, come on.'

Fifty-eight.

Another bounce, a glance at the bed, at the trapdoor under it. Then at the floor beside it, at the gap between the boards, eyes to a different gap between her feet. Wider, darker. Except for the eye, the bright, bright venomous green eye outlined on her HUD in a gold shimmer.

Breath caught, victory singing through her veins.

The McGuffin.

She grinned. 'Gotch'a.'

The eye blinked, narrowed, then shadowy fingers were pushing through the thin gap, squeezing then stretching. Hooking around the edges, gripping the space between her boots.

The tingle ripping up her nape.

She stamped on the fingers. Hard. Boards sagged beneath the

impact, fibres giving way. For a moment, she thought she'd be fine, that the old rotten wood would hold, and then she was through to her knee. Her thick, knee-high boots protected her calf from the splintered wood, her tough titanium-weave pants her knee.

Still holding the wand, both hands on the floor, the boards a vise around her kneecap, the inky darkness cold on her calf, the eye... The eye...

Lightning sparking off her vertebrae, burnt ozone filling the air.

Wrong wrong wrong.

Fuck fuck fuck.

A glance at Felix.

Eight-two percent. No way was she waiting another twelve for Mr Snarky Pants to help her out.

Mae heaved herself sideways, yanking her leg—

Hands on her ankle, the one lost to the dark.

Cold, cold, cold. Frost ripping through the leather boots, sinking through her skin.

On the HUD, her health falling, status messages boinging.

// Necrotic Grasp. Chill, movement slowed.

Well, hell.

And Felix... Staring straight ahead, the debugger at ninety-eight percent, the shadowy wings flickering.

Ninety-nine.

The hands climbing her calf, tightening around her knee. The chills climbed with them, infecting her torso, her arms, her hands. Fingers becoming ice blocks, elbows freezing.

Ninety-nine.

Ninety-nine.

Fumbling the wand, pointing it with a shaking hand.

Felix moving, Felix looking at her. Relief flooding her system, an additional surge of strength in her arms, heaving herself a little out of the hole.

Felix grinning, mouth open in a cat smile, wings strong and

dark, curling forward, curling *around* her: embracing.
  'You got it for me, Maggie.'
  She was yanked through the floor.

ACKNOWLEDGMENTS

Maggie was born in a deli, amidst overcooked roast chickens, soggy lettuce, sliced meat and endless piles of bacon. She grew up sandwiched between crows, polar bears and futuristic samurais, it's only now that her story gets the spotlight it deserves.

Usually, the thanks goes to my editor, friends and family, but for *Maggie* it all goes to the awesome, amazing and intrepid rebels (and plot bunny sympathisers) who helped to make *I Am Maggie Volume 1* happen. They are: Mike Dobey, Iris Juylyenne, Ian Chung, Jana M Evensong, David Holzborn, Heiko Koenig, Joe Lau, Cat Gardiner, Deanna Zinn, Scruffy Wizard, 'Will It Work', Dead Fish Books, Cinifang, Feral, Nicolas Lobotsky, Rhel na DecVande, Eric Cerevic, Mike Cody, K Hermans and Axel Kallesøe.

DON'T MISS ANOTHER BOOK!

I love keeping in touch with my readers, it's the second-best thing about being a writer (writing being the first best). Every fortnight (or thereabouts), I send out a newsletter with details about upcoming offers, new releases and extra special projects.

If you sign up for the mailing you'll receive exclusive behind-the-scenes extras, such as:

- free short stories
- deleted and alternate scenes from my books
- previews of upcoming books
- pancakes
- quizes
- and much, much more!

Scan the QR code or visit the link below to sign up.
belindacrawford.com/newsletter

ABOUT THE AUTHOR

Physics makes Belinda's brain hurt, while quadratics cause her eyes to cross and any mention of probability equations will have her running for the door. Nonetheless, she loves watching documentaries about the natural world, biology, space, history and technology.

She's also a sucker for a fast horse, a faster computer and superhero movies. When she's not doing the horse, computer or superhero thing, Belinda writes sci-fi and fantasy for readers who like their fiction action-packed, with diverse characters, butt-kicking heroines and complex worlds.

As a certified crazy horse person, when she's not wrangling six-legged dynamos on the page, she's wrangling four-legged powder-kegs in the paddock. Belinda brings that same certified craziness to her writing with the kind of unexpected twists that'll keep you guessing.

You can keep in touch with Belinda, or just pick her brains about sci-fi via her website, Facebook or by sending her an email (she loves email).

www.belindacrawford.com
belinda@belindacrawford.com

Have news delivered straight to your inbox
via her mailing list. Sign up at:
belindacrawford.com/newsletter